SUBDUE

A SCI-FI ALIEN WARRIOR ROMANCE

THE SKY CLAN OF THE TAORI
BOOK FOUR

TANA STONE

BROADMOOR BOOKS

For Bobbie Conway Hodges, with all my thanks for your support and inspiration

CHAPTER ONE

Naz

Before I was even aware of being conscious, I registered a dull ache all over, the pain rousing me. My recollections were hazy, but the last thing I'd seen as I'd taken the final escape pod off my sky ship had been laser fire tearing across the sky like cruel, red gashes. Then, there had been the bone-shaking explosion of my Taori vessel that had propelled me through the sky even faster. My heart squeezed at the painful memory, and I pressed a hand to my heart at the visceral pang, my fingers brushing the cool steel mesh of the sash crossing my chest.

The clanging of metal around my wrist made my hand pause. I brought my hands together, the heavy metal links rattling. Why was I in chains?

I sat up, peering through the darkness as my eyes adjusted.

Light trickled to me from a distance along with the sounds of more clanking chains accompanied by occasional groans. I swallowed, my throat dry and tight despite the damp, dank air that sent shivers sliding down my spine.

Where was I? Snatches of confusing images floating to the surface—spinning so fast in my escape pod that my head swam, then a hard jolt and pain, followed by scorching heat. But none of those impressions told me where I was now, or how I'd come to be there.

My gut churned. My crew. Where was my crew? Were they with me?

I could see and hear little, but that didn't mean my Taori brothers weren't also trapped in this dark place with me. They'd all ejected from the ship before me, although I held out small hope that every pod had landed safely.

Clearing my throat, I rasped, "Into the valley of death ride the Ten Thousand."

The words echoed back to me, even though my voice cracked. I waited for a beat, hoping to hear the response to the battle litany that I'd heard bellowed back so many times as I'd stood on the bridge of my ship. There was no response.

My shoulders sagged as I swung my feet from the hard bunk to the floor, the chains circling my ankles rattling. What kind of prison was this, and why was I there? My head throbbed, which I was sure had a lot to do with the gaping holes in my memory, and I tried to staunch the panic that welled up in me as I desperately tried to recall what had happened to me after I'd abandoned the sky ship.

I was the kalesh of my vessel, and my Taori warriors depended on me to lead them. When I'd seen that we would not be able to survive the alien attack, I'd promised my warriors that we would regroup and rise stronger than before. The Army of the Ten Thousand always rose from the ashes.

"Almost always," I allowed myself to whisper, even though the words felt traitorous on my lips. My father had been kalesh of a ship, and he had not been able to save his crew from a Sythian attack.

Even though we called ourselves The Immortals, we were not invulnerable to death. I knew that all too well, but I refused to let my father's fate be my own. I refused for that to be my legacy.

It was my destiny to save my crew, as I had many times before, and there was not a shred of doubt in my mind that I would do so again. I *had* to. But how could I keep this promise to myself and my crew—and save my family's legacy— if I was in chains with no memory?

Leaning forward on my hands, I released a low growl of frustration.

"I wouldn't make noise if I were you."

The voice, although it wasn't more than a furtive whisper, startled me. "Who is that?"

"It doesn't matter who I am. You don't want them to know you feel good enough to be making noises."

I straightened, trying to locate the voice. It was beyond my small cell, but not far. I stood and moved slowly and quietly toward the dimly illuminated bars. "Who are they?"

There was such a long silence, I feared the creature had been a figment of my addled imagination.

"You don't know where you are?"

"No. I remember nothing of how I got here."

An exhaled breath. "I shouldn't be shocked. They knocked you up pretty bad when they brought you in."

"Who are they?"

Another stretch of silence. "The guards and warden."

"This is a jail?"

"More like a waiting area. It's where they put us until we're ready for the arena. Some of us need to heal up after the beatings they give us, and some of us they're saving until they have no one else to offer up."

"The arena?"

"You don't remember being abducted and brought to the Xulonian moon?"

"I wasn't abducted." At least, I didn't think I was. "My ship was destroyed by the planet Xulon, and I ejected in an escape pod."

The creature made a tsk-ing sound. "If you landed here, then you have some bad luck. This is the combat moon, where they have alien slaves battle each other in a gladiator arena, while their most privileged citizens watch and place bets on who will live or die."

My stomach churned. "The battles are to the death?"

"That's right. You only leave the arena as a victor or a corpse."

This had not been what I'd been expecting, but it was only a stumbling block in my plan. If this was a fighting ring, then I would fight. I was a Taori, trained to battle against the most ferocious creatures in the universe. I'd been leading my crew across galaxies in pursuit of a vicious enemy—a Sythian swarm that devoured all in its path. If I could kill those bloodthirsty monsters, I could defeat some aliens in a fighting ring.

I grunted as I reformulated my plan. First, I would leave the arena as a victor, then, I would find and reassemble my crew, and finally, I would ensure that the aliens who'd attacked my sky ship and imprisoned me were punished for their crimes.

I growled again, hoping to lure the wardens to me. It was time to put the first part of my plan into motion.

After a few moments, I was rewarded with a guttural grunt from down the corridor. "You up, invader?"

Invader? Was that what they thought of me? Our ship

hadn't fired a single shot or sent even one threatening message at the planet when we'd jumped into its system, but even so, they'd attacked us without provocation. Now I was an invader?

I swallowed the fury that rose in the back of my throat, the rage as sharp and bitter as bile, and let loose a louder rumble that echoed off the stone walls and low ceiling. There were muffled grunts and murmurs in response, but no one spoke as heavy footsteps thudded toward me.

Although only scant light filtered in from the end of the corridor, I could make out the silhouette of the approaching guard, and my body tensed at the size of him. As a Taori, I was tall and broad-shouldered, with hard muscles honed from endless sessions in the training ring and on the battlefield. I towered over most other species, and my long tail and silver horns added to my impression as a predator to be feared.

But this creature... I swallowed hard and gritted my teeth as the bulk of the alien blocked the light, his tree-trunk legs set wide as he braced meaty hands on his hips.

"I assume you're one of the Xulonians who destroyed my ship."

The creature's belly shook as he laughed, the throaty rasp evolving into a hacking cough. "Me, a Xulonian? You should be so lucky." He leaned his head toward the bars, and I got a look at his gnarled face, sharp tusks jutting up from his protruding lower lip, and heavy-lidded, beady eyes glittering from within doughy folds of pale, laden flesh. "The Xulonians pay us well to do the jobs they can't."

I wasn't sure exactly what that meant—the Xulonians were clearly a vicious species, with no regard for the rules of combat or diplomacy, but maybe they preferred not to do their own dirty work. Regardless, it didn't change anything for me. The aliens who'd attacked my sky ship were still pulling the strings and commanding these guards. I had no problem taking them all down—as soon as I could fight my way free.

"I understand I'm here to fight."

The guard snorted and appraised me. "When you're ready."

I straightened to my full height and threw back my shoulders, the chains clanging around my ankles and wrists. "I am ready for any opponent you can muster."

Sounds of surprise rippled throughout the other cells, and the guard swung his head behind him to quell the noise before turning back to me. "The other fighters think you're either foolish or brave." His fleshy lips curled up into a menacing smile. "Or maybe you don't understand the rules."

I twitched up one shoulder. "I fight to the death. Am I missing anything?"

The creature glared at me for a beat, before throwing back his head and barking out a laugh. "You aren't missing anything, although there is a good chance you'll be missing something after you meet your first Kapanthian octo-beast."

"Like a leg," a low voice muttered from a nearby cell.

The guard ignored the other prisoner as he tilted his head at me. "The director wanted to wait until you were fully healed so the viewers could get the best possible fight, but who am I to stop you?" He backed up and fumbled with the iron bars. "You wish to die today?"

"I wish to fight. I have no plans to die."

"No one ever does," the guard said under his breath, as he swung the bars open and grasped me by the arm before I could shuffle forward.

As soon as his massive hand closed around my bicep, I knew that I would not be overpowering him solo, especially not with my hands and feet in heavy chains. As large and powerful as I was, this creature possessed brute force and bulk that wasn't easily matched without weapons. At the very least, I needed to lose my chains.

He jerked me forward and down the corridor, which gave me the chance to take in the dimly lit prison. Cells lined both sides of the arched corridor, but there were no windows to the outside. From the low ceiling that forced the guard to bend his head, to the moisture clinging to the dark stone, I was sure we were underground. When we reached the end of the cells, and he jerked me around a corner me in front of him and pushed me up a long ramp, I was certain of it.

The light that had barely reached the dank cells came from the wide, arched opening at the far end of the steep ramp. I blinked rapidly as my eyes balked at the brightness, but I stumbled forward. There was no question in my mind I was being taken to the fighting ring, and I breathed a sigh of relief that it was outside. I'd seen my fair share of underground battle rings, and I preferred my chances in an environment that was not shrouded in shadows.

At the top of the ramp, I paused as the guard yanked me to a stop and roughly unlocked the chains binding my ankles and feet. For a flicker of a moment, I considered turning on him, but I still didn't know how to escape from the underground prison. I suspected I wouldn't get far even if I could take him down.

"I would say I hope you don't get eaten alive," the guard said with a chuckle, "but I'd be lying."

Then he put a hand on my back and thrust me forward so that I staggered out into a bright arena, dust kicking up around my bare feet. Cheers rose from the stands that surrounded the round, open space, and I was startled to see that the creatures leaping to their feet had blistering red skin that appeared to be pulled taut over angular skulls. Were these the Xulonians?

I didn't have more than a beat to wonder about the spectators before I registered an enormous creature scuttling toward me on a collection of furry legs, sharp pincers glinting in the brutal sunlight. I dove to one side as a bladed pincer whizzed by my head and ruffled my long hair. Rolling to my feet, I jumped up into a battle crouch.

It was time to fight.

CHAPTER
TWO

Tyrria

"What do you think she is?"

The furtive question wasn't quiet enough to be considered a whisper, but the voice was soft and low, more curious than hostile. It was a question I'd heard enough over my lifetime that it no longer made me bristle, or even rush to wake.

"She's small, but she's not human."

"Not with that hair," another voice said, and I felt gentle fingers brush the long bangs that fell over my forehead. "It's pink."

"Lycithians have pink or purple hair."

"If she was Lycithian, wouldn't she have shifted into some kind of creature who wouldn't have been captured and brought here?"

This piqued my interest and stirred something within the recesses of my brain, sending panic fluttering in my stomach. I wasn't on the imperial transport anymore, and this wasn't the conversation of the other females en route to the empire's new colony.

I opened my eyes and sat up, causing the females around my bed to scurry back.

"She's not Lycithian. Not with those silver eyes."

I ignored the comments about my eyes. They were right. They weren't Lycithian, although I did get my hair from my Lycithian mother. Unfortunately, my Kayling father was the reason I couldn't shift at will like pure blood Lycithians—and the reason I had silver eyes. I pushed thoughts of both my mother and father aside as I assessed my current situation, my gaze quickly surveying the room.

Nope, definitely not a transport ship.

Although the transport I'd been a passenger on had been suitably equipped, it had been far from luxurious. My quarters had been utilitarian—all dull metal and hard surfaces, with tight corridors that echoed the heavy footfall of the security officers who'd patrolled them. This wasn't that.

The ceiling in the spacious room was high and domed, with light sifting in from the multicolored glass above, and sending slats of rainbow light to dapple the gleaming floors. Aside from being bright, the round room was dotted with chaise lounges upholstered in shimmery fabric and piled with cushions. Sheer panels of fabric hung from various points in the room and were tied back to marble columns with gilded tassels.

"Where am I?" I asked one of the females stretched across a nearby chaise.

She arched a dark eyebrow, which was in dramatic contrast with her flaxen hair. "You don't know?"

I shook my head, which felt heavy, remembering that the last time I'd felt so woozy I'd been coming out of being drugged by the Hettite slavers who'd taken me and the other females from the transport.

I swung my head around to see if there were any of the lumbering, tusked creatures lurking in this place, but there were none. That was something. But another glance also told me that there were none of the other women who'd been with me on the transport. I hadn't spent much time with the security officers or scientists who'd been abducted with me, but at least they would have been someone I'd recognized. As it was, the females surrounding me were total strangers.

I tried not to think about where the other women from the transport had been sent, but my gut tightened at the very real possibility that I'd never see them again. For some strange reason, this made tears burn behind my eyelids, and I blinked them away quickly.

"You're on the battle moon, sweetie." A female with wide, doe eyes knelt beside me, putting a hand on my arm. "You've been recruited to be one of the attendants."

"Recruited?" I scoffed. "I was kidnapped."

A brunette put a finger to her lips. "We don't talk about how we all came to be here." She flicked her gaze around, as if someone was watching. "They don't like it."

Tendrils of fear curled sharp talons around my heart as I looked back to the wide-eyed female by my side, and the metal collar clamped around her neck. Tiny blue lights were embedded around it and blinked rhythmically. I raised a hand to my own neck, my fingers touching the cool metal ringing my own throat. "They?"

The female lounging nearby let out an exasperated sigh and sat up. "This is the Xulonian battle moon, and we've all been chosen to take care of the fighters who battle it out in the arena. Consider yourself lucky that you aren't running for your life on the hunting moon."

Vague memories of a red-skinned alien talking about his people's pleasure moons floated into my mind, but it was more of a hazy nightmare than a clear recollection. I curled my fingers around my metal collar but the female kneeling beside me grabbed my hand and shook her head. "Don't pull it unless you want to get a shock."

"A shock?" I repeated in disbelief.

"You don't think they'd give us free rein around the arena without some way to keep us from fleeing, do you?" The blonde with dark brows raised them again, but her voice had softened. "As long as you don't try to escape or take it off, you won't get zapped." She feathered her own pink, painted fingernails to her collar. "Think of it as jewelry you never take off."

I fought the urge to claw at my neck and tear the metal from my skin. Even though I'd been on my way to the outpost to be the companion to an imperial commander, I hadn't been forced to do it. I'd agreed to the deal to improve the Kaylings' status with the empire, a sacrifice my father had convinced me would finally make me a valued member of the species.

I frowned as I thought about my father, and my frown melted when my mind turned to my mother. She never would have allowed me to be sent off to be some whore for the empire, even if her species was highly valued as pleasurers. She'd never worked as one, and I was sure that if she'd lived past my sixth birthday, she wouldn't have allowed me to be used as a pawn by the Kayling. But when she was alive, we hadn't lived on the Kayling home world, and she hadn't experienced their fear of what they didn't understand. She'd never viewed my mixed heritage as anything to hide, probably because she didn't know what it was like to not fit fully anywhere.

The only good thing to come out of living most of my life on Kayling surrounded by a species who considered me strange and not to be trusted was that I wasn't easily rattled by new situations. I'd learned to become a chameleon to adapt, embracing as much of my Kayling heritage as I could, even though in my heart, I wished I was fully Lycithian. Partly, so I could have morphed into a fierce monster anytime one of the Kaylings whispered about my mixed blood, but also so I would have no connection to the father who'd agreed to use his own daughter as a political pawn.

"There aren't many rules around here." The woman beside me released her grip on my hands and smiled as I forced myself to relax. "The collars mean we can go wherever we want within the complex, which is handy, when you're attending to one of the fighters."

"Attending to?"

The blonde shook her head as if anticipating my concern. "This isn't the lust moon. Our job is to bathe them and bring them food."

"Basically, help them heal up after their battles and prep them for the next ones," another woman added, flipping her black braids off her shoulder. "Not that they don't sometimes require more."

The female next to me patted my arm. "But not all of them. Usually, they're too exhausted or wounded to do anything but collapse."

"Usually," the blonde drawled with a wicked smile. "But only the fighters who've won more than once get an attendant, and not many keep winning, so it's rare to be with a fighter for long."

I flinched at this. "What happens when they lose?"

"They lose, they die," the female with braid said. "The Xulonians pay to watch aliens battle to the death."

"My best advice?" The blonde pinned me with a serious look. "Don't get attached. None of the fighters last forever, and if you fall for one, it will break your heart when they bring you their mangled body. Trust me." Her eyes registered pain for a beat. "Don't convince yourself that this is anything but a twisted game that we can't escape."

"You don't need to scare her," the woman next to me said, shooting the others scathing looks. "She just arrived."

She didn't need to worry about me, and neither did the blonde. I'd learned a while ago not to trust males. Getting close to someone only meant you would eventually get hurt, and I didn't plan to open myself to that kind of pain again anytime soon.

"I'm fine." I straightened and squared my shoulders. "And I'm not the kind of girl who's going to fall for an alien fighter."

Now that I understood the ground rules, I was able to focus my mind on surviving. Despite what these females believed, I couldn't accept that there was no way off the battle moon. All I had to do was stay alive and look for the weaknesses in the system.

And hope my Lycithian shapeshifting decides to kick in, I thought darkly. Even though I had the shape-shifting gene, my abilities were erratic at best. I'd only been able to morph a few times and it had happened randomly, much to the shock of the Kaylings who'd found themselves talking to me one moment and a fluffy, long-toed windernutter the next. Turning into a pink creature the size of a house cat with unusually long toes would not exactly help me escape from the battle moon, even if I could will it to happen. Now, if I could shift into a deadly beast, that would be another matter altogether.

As I was imagining what kind of creature I'd love to shift into, the door at the far end of the room slid open, and a pair of burly, tusked aliens entered. I cringed at the sight of them, although a part of me was glad they weren't the red-skinned Xulonians who'd reminded me of demons from my nightmares.

"New girl," one of them barked, pointing a stubby finger at me.

I stood, my knees wobbling even as I faced them defiantly. "My name is Tyrria."

The guard snorted derisively. "Whatever. Come with us."

I hesitated, and he slid his hand down the long baton in his hand.

One of the women gave me a small shove. "You should do what they say."

I moved forward before the guard's thumb could press the button that I suspected would give me a painful shock. "I'm coming."

I fell in step between the two hulking creatures, giving a last glance back at the sumptuous, light-filled room. "Where am I going?"

"A new fighter just won a battle. It's time for you to go to work."

I gulped as they led me down a hall with high ceilings and pale-yellow walls, my nerves jangling at the thought of the kind of alien who could win in a fight to the death. "You sure you want me, and not one of the more experienced attendants?"

The guard in back choked back a laugh as they paused in front of a door. "There's no better way to break a new girl in than with a beast like him."

Beast? I opened my mouth, but any complaints or questions died on my lips as the door was opened, and I was shoved into the room where a creature stood, dripping with blood, and heaving in ragged breaths.

CHAPTER
THREE

Naz

I sucked in hot breath as I stood in the dusty arena, with cheers swelling around me. The deafening noise reverberated through my body, rising and falling like a Taori battle cry. My heart pounded in time to the adulation as I stared down at the blood pooling in the hardpacked dirt at my feet. The blood might have been green when it came from the hulking beast with many legs and snapping pincers, but now it appeared almost black as it ran in rivulets from the limp body.

I stepped back to keep my bare feet from being coated in the sticky blood, as they were already caked with dirt. A trail of my own red blood trickled down one leg, mixing with sweat until it was more clear than crimson when it reached my ankle. I grunted as I glanced at the thin cut slicing across the outside of my thigh, a souvenir from my quick opponent and its razor-sharp pincers. It wasn't deep, and it would heal, whereas the alien creature lying motionless on its side would not.

I flinched when a thick hand closed over my arm, jerking toward the guard, and almost lunging at him from instinct.

He pressed a pointed spear to my side. "Save it for your next fight."

I allowed my shoulders to sag. The fight was over, and I'd won. I tipped my head up to truly take in the arena, as I was prodded toward the wide door that would take me back to the cells. I hadn't had more than a few moments to observe the place where I'd fought. I'd been too distracted by the terrifying beast attacking me, with flashing blades for hands and more legs than I could count or track.

I'd already seen that the spectators were red-skinned aliens with deep-set eyes and thin limbs that appeared almost like sticks as they waved them in the air. Their mouths were like dark, vacuous holes as they screamed, and the fact that they were cheering for me, and my bloody kill, only made a shudder of revulsion spasm down my spine. They were packed tightly into the stands that encircled the dirt-floored arena, and a clear dome appeared to shield the structure from the heat of the blinding sun. Colorful strings of pennants were strung across the fighting area, the colors faded with dust and age.

How long had the arena been standing? It looked ancient, but I knew better than to rely on my eyes alone. The stone walls leading to the spectator stands reached higher than I could leap, but they could be weathered to appear old, as could the dingy iron bars that had guarded the subterranean cells. The alternative—that the aliens who'd attacked my ship had also been abducting aliens and using them in brutal gladiator fights for generations—was a horrific possibility.

"Move!" A sharp sting from the guard's spear brought my attention back to him, and I walked forward.

The cheers became rhythmic as I moved toward the arched opening that would return me to darkness, and I realized that they were chanting "beast" at me. Was I the beast?

Glancing down at my own bare chest that was marked with dark ink that charted my journey across the skies and the battles I'd led, I saw that it was smeared with the green blood of my victim. Droplets clung to the steel mesh sash crossing my chest and splattered the snug, black shorts that were the only clothing I wore.

I snuck a glance at one of the crowd as I walked closer to the edge of the arena. The alien's black eyes were wide, and his lipless mouth curled up in a petrified smile as he cheered for me. To this creature, my silver horns, long tail, and darkly inked skin must make me seem like a ferocious beast. Even before I'd torn my opponent's legs from his body and snapped his neck.

Still, I was not the species that was abducting others so I could force them to kill each other for their amusement. I was not the one who'd destroyed a ship and scattered the crew without provocation. I was not the one without honor.

I met the alien's eyes, narrowing my own in fury and determination. Now that I'd seen my attackers and abductors I was even more resolved to make them pay for what they'd done to my crew, and what they were doing to every innocent alien creature they believed was expendable.

"You will pay for your craven bloodlust, and your blood will run like a river racing to the sea," I said under my breath as I held the Xulonian's gaze.

His cheering stopped, and his expression froze, his arms dropping like a marionette with its strings cut. He hadn't heard my words, but he had no doubt seen the hatred in my gaze. I gave a slight nod as if to tell him that his fear was correct. I was coming for him. The Taori were coming for all of them.

"Keep moving, *beast*." The guard gave me a rough push from behind, snorting out a guttural laugh as he repeated the chant of the spectators.

I ignored his taunt. I didn't care if they called me a beast. I would be a beast, if it meant surviving and finding my crew again. It would take a beast to stay alive in this cruel alien world, and I had no choice but to stay alive so I could fulfill my promise to my Taori brothers and reunite us.

As the lumbering guard pushed me through the arched opening, the cheering became muffled, and the bright light was consumed by the darkness. The heat that had warmed my skin was replaced by a dank chill that slid across my flesh like a shroud, and I no longer breathed in the scent of sweat and dust. Now the only smells that filled my nostrils were of mold and fear.

Another guard met us, grunting as he took the position in front of me and leading us down the long corridor. I waited for the water to drip on me from the slick stones overhead as we descended deeper, but instead we started to go up.

"Where are we going?" I didn't want them to hear the alarm in my voice, as I contemplated where they might be taking me, if not back to my cell to await another fight. Had the other prisoner been wrong? Were the victors rewarded with a different kind of punishment—or death?

"You won," the guard in front said, without turning his thick head. "Winners don't stay in the dungeons."

I allowed myself a relieved breath. I'd been in worse places than the cell I'd woken in, but I would not miss the darkness and the oppressive feel of despair that had emanated from the stones themselves.

"The crowds liked you," the other guard added. "They'll wager big on your next match, so the director will want you rested and well-fed."

As if I'd just remembered that I hadn't eaten a bite since I'd been on my ship, my stomach growled. I was no less devoted to killing all of them, but I would welcome a meal before I did so.

The dark stone of the underground corridors gave way to hallways that sloped up, and finally to high ceilings and tall windows. The light was almost as bright as in the arena, although the glass was mottled and tinted with color, so I couldn't see outside. Still, I was grateful to see the colored light dancing across the floor as my dirty feet slapped the pale stones and left bloody footprints in my wake.

We stopped in front of a broad door, and the first guard shoved it open, while the one behind me pushed me through. I stumbled a few steps before righting myself, and turning to see them pulling it closed again with malicious grins.

"Enjoy it while you can, beast. You might not be so lucky in your next fight."

Then the door thudded closed.

I swiveled around, gaping at the room that had replaced the fetid cell and wondering if I was imagining it. Light streamed in from a domed ceiling made of the same mottled, vividly hued glass as the windows in the hallway, dappling the gleaming, sand-colored floor. Tucked in one alcove was a round, sunken pool, with steam rising from its surface, and in another was a large, round bed piled with cushions. But it was the table in the center of the room that drew my attention.

Round, and laden with plates topped with domed covers, the table held savory scents that left me in no doubt as to what was beneath the covers. Multi-tiered stands were stacked high with colorful sweets that my nose could detect even from across the room. I knew I should bathe the dirt and blood from my skin before eating, but my hunger drove all civilized thoughts from my mind.

Before I could descend on the table and devour the food,

the door behind me opened again. If I was going to be taken from the room for another fight before I'd eaten, they would not find me so reasonable. I swung around, my chest heaving as I prepared to resist.

Instead of the two heavy-set, tusked guards who had escorted me to the room, a small female with short, pink hair stumbled inside, and came to a stop in front of me. The doors slammed again, and we were left alone.

The female's silver eyes widened as she looked me up and down. I instinctively drew myself up to my full height, in preparation of introducing myself as Kalesh Naz of the Taori, my swishing tail slowing behind me, and my steel mesh sash rattling as a deep rumble vibrated my chest. Then, her eyes rolled back in her head, and I lunged forward to catch her before she collapsed to the floor.

CHAPTER FOUR

Tyrria

My nose twitched, the metallic scent of blood making me jerk my head.

"You should not move." The voice was a low purr that held no threat, but I stiffened nonetheless.

Opening my eyes, a face swam into view. Dark hair with silver at the temples, striped horns curling around his ears, scruff dusting his cheeks, and eyes so iridescent blue they seemed to glow. The face I'd seen before I'd been overcome with a wave of dizziness and my knees had buckled.

"What are you?" I'd meant to say, 'who are you?' but my brain was still sluggish, and I'd never seen a creature like him before.

He tilted his head at me, his gaze moving across the hair that fell across my forehead. "What are *you*?"

I started to bristle at the question he returned to me, since it was one I'd heard all my life, but I had been the one to ask first. I couldn't exactly get my feathers ruffled if I'd asked the exact thing of him. Besides, if I'd never laid eyes on his species, chances were good he'd never met a Lycithian or a Kayling.

"I'm half Lycithian and half Kayling." I realized that I was lying in the creature's lap, and I tried to sit up. "My name is Tyrria."

Dizziness rolled through me again, and I sank back into his lap.

"I am Kalesh Naz of the Sky Clan of the Taori."

I blinked quickly and tried to remember the words. "Do you want me to say all of that when I address you?"

"You do not need to address me formally. We are not on the command deck of my sky ship."

I released a sigh. "Good. I'll call you Kalesh."

The corners of his mouth quivered. "As you wish, Tyrria." Then he eyed me seriously, as I tried to push myself up on my elbows, my arms trembling. "You fainted. You should not try to move."

I vaguely remembered being pushed into a room and spotting him covered in dark tattoos, dirt, and two colors of blood. I slid my gaze to the metal mesh that crossed his heavily inked chest and was smeared with blood, my nose wrinkling. "You're one of the fighters."

He grunted, his brow furrowing.

I remembered that I was supposed to be attending to him, not slumped on the ground being tended to by him. "I'm supposed to be taking care of you."

He cut his eyes down the length of my body. "You?"

I scowled at him, my irritation overcoming any lightheadedness. "Why not me?"

He shrugged one shoulder. "I do not need to be taken care

of. I am the kalesh of my crew. I take care of my Taori brothers." Then he inclined his head again. "And you are very small."

I sat up quickly, forcing him to lean back to avoid our heads bumping. I waved a hand at him. "Only compared to a..."

His brows lifted, although his expression darkened as he released me. "A beast like me?"

I clamped my mouth shut. I'd been about to call him a beast, but I wasn't about to admit that now. "I was going to call you a massive Taobi."

"Taori," he corrected, his mouth twitching.

I scooted away from him, taking in the fact that he wore only snug, black shorts and was coated in a layer of dust that was probably on me now. "I've never heard of the Taori."

"And I am sorry to say that I have never heard of the Lycithians or the Kaylings, but my people don't come from this galaxy. Or this time."

Now, I lifted a brow. "You don't come from this time?"

He readjusted himself so that he knelt on his knees, his hands braced on his thighs. His long, fur-tipped tail curled behind him on the floor, and I was glad to be distracted by that, instead of the considerable lump in his shorts.

"My sky ship was pulled through a temporal wormhole, and ended up in the Xulonian system, five hundred years in the future."

I snapped my gaze back to his face, searching for signs of deception or madness. "You come from half a millennium in the past? Are you sure?"

He nodded grimly. "Our science officer and our instruments confirmed it. Also, the technology the Xulonians used to destroy our ship was like nothing we had seen before. In our time, we are considered advanced in our technology. Here, we were outmatched to the point that we appeared primitive."

His words seemed sincere, as did his face when he related

the story. I'd heard of temporal wormholes. I'd just never encountered anyone who'd been pulled through one.

I brushed some dirt from my arm. "Pretty rotten luck to end up near Xulon. The one thing I knew about them before being abducted was that they're wildly xenophobic."

The Taori's pupils flared. "You were abducted?"

I almost laughed. "Well, I didn't volunteer to be taken to a battle moon so I could attend to victorious alien fighters." I thought of what the Xulonian had said when I was on the Hettite ship, and what the other females had said when I'd woken up here. "At least I'm not on the hunting moon, or the lust moon."

The alien frowned. "There are other moons where the Xulonians use captured aliens for amusement?"

I nodded. This guy really didn't know anything. "If you don't know about the moons, how did you end up on one?"

"When our ship was destroyed, I was the last Taori to escape in one of our pods. I must have crashed here, but I haven't seen any others of my crew."

"If they were in escape pods, maybe they landed on the other moons." I didn't want to suggest that they'd already been purged in the arena. If his crew members were as huge and fierce as he appeared to be, maybe they wouldn't be defeated so easily, either.

He stood quickly, curling his hands into fists as he paced beside me. "If they are on other moons, I will need to find them."

"Find them? On other moons?" Now I suspected he might be mad, after all. "You're trapped on this one. We both are."

He flicked a look at me. "I will not remain here for long. It is my destiny to reunite my crew and return to our time. We are the Immortal Army of the Ten Thousand, and we will complete our mission."

This alien sure did have a lot of titles. I was glad I only had to remember Kalesh.

"How do you plan to do that when there are armed guards everywhere?" I looked at his neck, raising my fingers to the metal collar circling mine. "At least you don't have to worry about one of these."

The alien swung his gaze to me, his eyes locking onto the collar. "That is not jewelry customary to your species?"

"An electrified collar that can immobilize or hurt me if I try to escape?" I narrowed my eyes at him. "No, this is what the Xulonians put on all the female attendants, so we can move freely around the arena complex to get things for the fighters without risk of escaping."

The Taori's ice-blue eyes glittered with fire as he knelt beside me, touching the collar with a gentleness that was surprising considering his size and ferocious appearance. "I will free you from this, Tyrria."

A shiver went down my spine at the sound of my name on his lips. I met his gaze as it blazed with an intensity that made my breath catch in my chest. Clearing my throat, I scooted back from him. "Don't make promises you can't keep."

"I am Taori," he told me in a velvety growl. "I never break a vow."

I tore my gaze from his, my heart pounding as I touched the metal around my neck where it had been warmed by his fingers. I knew better than to trust a male. Even my own father, who should have protected me above all others, had betrayed me. It was foolish to think that this stranger—a creature who looked almost like a beast—would save me when no one else ever had.

You can only rely on yourself, Tyrria. Believing in the Taori will only bring you heartache.

"I don't need a vow from you, Kalesh," I said when my breath had steadied. "I only need you to keep winning."

As brutal as he looked covered in blood and grime, I suspected there were much scarier fighters whom I wouldn't want to attend.

He opened his mouth before reconsidering what he was going to say and giving me a single nod as he stood and towered over me. "Then our desires are aligned."

CHAPTER FIVE

Naz

I liked hearing her call me Kalesh, even though it would have been considered a formal greeting on Taor. Her voice was soft, but her words were certain, and when she locked her silver eyes on me my heart lurched in my chest.

What I didn't like was the resigned look on her face when she'd told me the only thing she needed from me was for me to continue winning. She didn't trust me. Not yet.

I brushed this aside, telling myself that she didn't know of the Taori so she couldn't know that we did not break our vows, or that we always completed our missions. Now that I'd promised to free her from the bondage of the Xulonians' battle moon, she was part of my mission.

Foolish, a little voice husked in the back of my brain. *You should not have made such a vow. Not when your obligation is to find your crew and reunite them. Not when your legacy as kalesh is at stake. An alien female will only slow you down and keep you from a quick escape.*

I gave my head a firm shake, banishing these thoughts. I didn't know why I'd made a promise to save a creature I barely knew, but now that I'd uttered the words I was bound to them like a planet bound to its sun. I could no more fail her than I could fail my Taori brothers. I would have to save us all.

I chanced a glance at Tyrria as she sat beneath me, her fingers still touching the studded metal collar ringing her neck. I had no idea what it meant to be half Lycithian and half Kayling, but I did know that it was hard for me to look away from her. She was small compared to me, but she was long-limbed and moved much like the pleasurers I'd known who were skilled dancers. Despite her tendency to hide her eyes behind the long sweep of pale pink hair that she wore across her forehead, her silver gaze was shrewd and penetrating. I wondered if she moved like a pleasurer in all ways, or what her eyes were like when she was in the throes of passion.

Do not even think about it, I told myself as I turned away from her and walked purposefully toward the table of food. My priority was to escape. Anything else—even if it was in the form of a beautiful female—was a distraction I couldn't afford.

"Wait!"

Tyrria's voice stopped me before I reached the table of food. "I think I'm supposed to serve you."

I glanced over my shoulder as I resumed my walk. "I do not need to be served." I snatched a beige puff of dough that was dusted with something blue and powdery and popped it into my mouth. Sweetness exploded across my tongue, and I moaned at the rush of flavor. Taori food—especially that we ate on our sky ship—tended to be the type of rations that would keep in a hold for many rotations—bland and hearty. This food was anything but that.

I plucked a dome off a plate, and a cloud of savory steam filled the air. I barely waited to see what was underneath the steam before grabbing some and lifting it to my lips. The fried meat of some kind crackled in my mouth as I chewed, the saltiness welcome after the sweet. I continued to eat, only pausing to pour myself a goblet of a claret-colored drink and downing it in a single gulp.

"This definitely isn't helping your overall look," Tyrria said, as she joined me at the table, her gaze darting to the drops of grease that had dripped on my chest and the blue powder now dusting the smeared blood.

She shook her head and let out an exasperated breath. "You may not want someone to serve you, but you definitely need some help cleaning up. From what the other females told me, I'm supposed to clean you up after your fights and tend to any wounds." She cut a pointed gaze to my leg and then reached for my mesh sash. "At least let me take this off you so it doesn't get covered in food."

Her hands brushed my skin as she lifted the mesh from my skin, and heat sizzled over my flesh. She stretched her arms high, but she wasn't tall enough to slip it over my head.

She huffed out a breath, irritated either at herself or at me or both. "Can you bend down a bit?"

I complied, bending my knees until she could lift the sash over my head, but that also meant that her chest was now at my eye level, and she had leaned close enough that it was impossible for me not to breathe in her scent. The sweet, feminine aroma of her forced a pained moan from my lips as my heart hammered and my body flushed with scorching heat.

Startled, she dropped the sash and it hit my shoulder and bounced to the floor. Before she could back away from me, I'd curled my tail around her legs and wrapped my arms around her waist, lifting her from the ground. I blindly strode to the nearest wall and pressed her against it, my body moving as if by instinct and not by my command.

"Kalesh," she gasped, as I covered her body with mine, burying my face in her neck and greedily sucking in the intoxicating scent of her. When I didn't respond, she beat her hands on my shoulders. "Kalesh Naz of the Taori!"

Her words were like cold water dousing my fervor, and I jerked back, releasing her and staring at the female as she gaped at me like I was deranged. I staggered back, raking a hand through my hair and trying to shake off the haze of desire that had consumed me. The last time I'd experienced such a powerful bout of lust...

My blood, which had been burning hot within my veins, went cold. I should not be close to going through the Taori mating fever we called the Quaibyn, but I also remembered my science officer warning that the temporal worm hole could cause the fever to strike any of us. I squeezed my eyes closed, hoping to shut out the reality of what had happened. I'd just felt the first stirring of a mating fever that could only be cured one way. And if I didn't quench my desire by mating with a female, the fever would only get worse until it drove me mad.

"Apologies," I rasped without opening my eyes or looking at Tyrria. "I am not feeling like myself."

"It's fine," Tyrria said. "I shouldn't have taken off your sash without asking."

I shook my head vigorously. "It was not your fault. I do not feel well."

The words sounded hollow because they were lies. I knew I was not ill. Not in the way she would think. This was exactly how all my bouts with the Quaibyn had started. The fever affected each Taori male differently, and the hallmark of mine was that I was so consumed by my desire that I became unaware of my actions. It was like the fever took over and the disciplined kalesh vanished, replaced by a lust-fueled creature who only cared about his carnal desires—or drawing blood.

I would become what they thought I was—a beast.

CHAPTER SIX

Tyrria

It took me a moment to gather my breath as he stalked away from me. What had just happened? One moment the Taori was stuffing his face and the next he was pinning me against the wall and smelling me like I was the one covered in sugar.

Was it like he claimed, and he didn't feel well? I scrunched my lips to one side as I eyed his broad back. If it was an illness, it had come over him quicker than any sickness I'd heard of, and the only symptoms I could see looked a lot like a guy being aroused. I might not know much about alien illness, but I'd known enough males to know when one wanted me.

My skin went cold as I thought about the hungry looks the Kayling males had given me growing up. They might not have accepted me as one of them because of my Lycithian blood, but that didn't mean they didn't want to see if the rumors about

Lycithian females were true. I swallowed down my revulsion at the memories of their hot gazes, my own gaze never leaving the Taori.

Even though he was an alien who had all the physical markings of a primitive brute, he'd seemed to be civilized when he'd talked to me. Unlike the Kayling males of my childhood, he hadn't looked at me like I was a meal to be devoured. He hadn't even tried to take advantage of my position as his attendant or pressed his advantage as a victorious fighter. Until I'd taken off his metal sash, and he'd snapped.

I could still feel where his tail had coiled around my legs, and the skin on my neck tingled—flesh memory from his lips feathering warm breath across my throat and sending tremors down my spine. As startled as I'd been by him nearly pouncing on me, I was more startled by my body's own traitorous reaction. Instead of being repulsed like I'd been with every unwanted leer from a Kayling, my heart had stuttered in my chest, and my nipples had hardened as he'd pressed his bare chest into me. He might look more threatening than any Kayling, but my body hadn't reacted with fear. I might have been shocked, but I'd also been secretly thrilled.

Seriously, Tyrria? I almost rolled my eyes at myself. *You get pinned to the wall by an alien with horns and a tail who's covered in blood because he just killed someone in the battle ring, and you aren't scared?*

My self-preservation instinct, which I'd thought was well-honed after a lifetime of having to look after myself—must be short-circuiting, if I was attracted to the Taori and not running for my life. I eyed his heaving back. Despite how he looked, and what he'd just done, I couldn't convince myself that I was in danger from him. Every instinct in me said that Kalesh was safe.

I huffed out a breath, exasperated by my own naïveté. Even

if I was right, and the Taori wasn't a danger to me, the last thing I needed was to be distracted by him—or my own response to him. He might profess to want to get me away from the battle moon with him, but how did I know he was as true to his word as he claimed? So far, his grasp on his own self-control seemed tenuous.

The fact remained that I didn't know Kalesh. I knew that his touch scorched my skin and made my heart race. I also knew that my gut told me that he wasn't like all the other males I'd known. But the one thing I knew above all of this was that I could only rely on myself.

"Have you eaten?"

The Taori's voice drew my attention to him again, and I was surprised that he sounded as calm and steady as he had before he'd grabbed me. He craned his head to look at me, his crystal-blue eyes no longer manic and fiery. Whatever illness had come over him must have passed just as quickly.

I put a hand to my stomach, feeling the ache of hunger that I'd been too distracted to notice before. "Not in a while."

He motioned with his head for me to join him at the table.

"I'm not sure if I'm supposed to eat your food." I glanced at the door, as if one of the grotesque guards might come lumbering in to slap my hands from the food.

"You said you're my attendant, yes?"

I nodded.

"And your job is to attend to my wants?"

I moved my head up and down, but this time more warily.

The Taori swept an arm across the display on the table. "Then I want you to join me in eating."

I walked slowly toward him, my gaze never leaving the alien, even though he seemed relaxed and focused on the culinary offerings, as he piled a plate with food. Even though there was almost no hint of the creature who'd taken me in his arms so quickly and forcefully that I'd barely had time to snatch a breath, I maneuvered myself, so that I was standing on the other side of the round table.

Kalesh raised his eyes, and his lips curled into a half smile, but he returned his focus to the food as I did the same, filling a plate with all sorts of savory and sweet morsels. Instead of taking his plate and goblet to the empty table flanked by four high-backed chairs, the Taori strode to a sunken area covered in a thick, colorfully patterned rug. He sank down and criss-crossed his legs with his plate and goblet in front of him.

"It's been a long time since I dined like my ancestors did when they fought battles across the plains of Taor." He braced a pair of large cushions behind his back. "As much as I value my sky ship," his face contorted in pain for a beat, "*valued* my sky ship, I am glad for a respite from all the cold steel."

I took a seat across from him, popping food into my mouth almost before I'd sat down fully. After a few bites, I washed it all down with a generous swallow of the alien wine. "You consider being imprisoned on a battle moon and forced to fight to the death a respite?"

He shrugged. "I do not know why I am here, but I do know that my fate was etched in the fabric of the sky—as was yours. Even our meeting was written in the stars. It is all a part of our stories that are being stitched into immortality." He swept his gaze across the sumptuous room. "Our stories do not end here, but I do not mind enjoying the small pleasures this chapter brings me."

Kalesh locked eyes with me, and my mouth went dry. Why did I have a sense that he meant me when he said small pleasures, and even more crucially, why did a part of me thrill at that thought?

We stared at each other in silence until the door swung open, breaking the spell and allowing me to release a breath.

Two of the hulking guards thundered into the room, their eyes widening when they spotted us sitting together on the floor and eating.

"He's still covered in blood," one of them said, as much to his colleague as to us. "He's not ready to fight again."

The other guard grunted, extending a hand and pointing at me. "You're supposed to get him ready for the next fight. That means clean him up and make him look like a champion." His top lip curled up malevolently. "Or we'll get him a new girl who knows how to attend to a fighter."

Kalesh stood. "I do not want a new girl. This one will do the job."

"See that she does," the first guard said with a snort. "You fight again soon—and your next opponent won't be so easy to kill."

CHAPTER SEVEN

Naz

The door rattled when it slammed shut behind the guards. Even though their threat of an impending fight made my stomach clench, I didn't want to focus on the arduous task ahead. If I thought of the odds against what I was determined to do—win every fight until I could escape, track down my crew, punish the Xulonians for their cruelty, and leave this galaxy and this time so we could resume the hunt for the Sythians in our own time—I might lose hope. But a Taori never lost hope and never gave up. We were the Immortals. I forced thoughts of my father's fate from my mind. His fate would not be mine. It *could* not.

"Into the valley of death ride the Ten Thousand," I whispered to myself, hearing the words, 'We are the Taori. We are the Immortals' in my head, as if my crew was bellowing them back to me as they always had.

"What?" Tyrria wrenched her gaze from the closed door, as if she expected the guards to burst back inside.

I shook my head as I grabbed the last bread crust from my plate and devoured it in a single bite. "You should finish eating while I do as they wish."

I didn't wait for a response, striding toward the sunken pool with steam rising from the bubbling surface and peeling the close-fitting black shorts from my body. I stepped from them and left them in a pile on the floor, before swinging myself into the water. The heat enveloped me and stung my skin for a moment before I adjusted to the temperature. The gash on my leg burned, but I pushed through the pain, knowing that the wound needed to be cleaned, anyway.

Once I'd grown accustomed to the hot water, and my cut had stopped burning, I sank down so that everything up to my shoulders was submerged. I released a moan as my muscles uncoiled, breathing in the perfumed steam that held notes of musk and spice.

There were advantages to winning, although I despised having to kill other captives to stay alive. I pushed aside that thought, reminding myself that I'd been responsible for much death in my long lifetime, although none of the deaths of the Sythians had been undeserved.

"Here, let me wash your back." Tyrria's voice behind me made me jump.

I hadn't heard her rise from the floor and walk over to the pool, but I'd been so focused on luxuriating in the water that my guard had been lowered. "You don't have to—"

"Will you stop being such a stubborn ass?" She let out a tortured sigh. "You heard the guards. If I don't do a good job, they'll find someone who will. So back up and let me scrub your back."

I'd heard the guards, but I also knew what had happened

the last time she'd touched me. My better judgment warred with my overconfidence, as I reassured myself that I could control the fever now that I knew it had begun.

As if you've ever controlled the fever when it consumes you, I thought darkly. But Tyrria was right. The guards were watching, and I doubted they would hesitate to remove her if she was found wanting. I didn't know the fate of an attendant who failed at her task, but I suspected it wasn't good.

Even though I had no need of a female to take care of me, I did feel a powerful pull toward the half Lycithian-half Kayling. I hadn't allowed myself to desire anything for so long that the sensation was strange, but I also knew I couldn't give her up. Especially since I'd vowed to take her with me when I escaped.

With a sigh of my own, I did as Tyrria requested, moving back in the water until I brushed the side of the sunken pool but keeping my eyes facing forward. She drew in a sharp breath as she dipped a fluffy cloth into the water and placed it on my shoulder.

"Wow, that's hot."

I bit my bottom lip as she rubbed the cloth across my back and down each shoulder, saying a prayer of gratitude to the old gods that there was wet fabric between our skin. Already, my flesh was warming from her closeness, and my heart thudded in my ribcage. If she touched me, I might lose control again.

"Can you stand up a bit? I need to reach your lower back."

I steeled myself as I stood and the water sluiced off my body, carrying dirt and blood that tinged the water and swirled to the bottom. Now that I was standing, the water only reached the top of my ass where my tail emerged, although I fought to keep my tail under the surface and still. The faster my heart raced, the more my tail longed to twitch as if I was stalking prey.

But Tyrria wasn't my prey. She was the female I'd promised

to save, so I pressed my lips together in a hard line and forced myself to breathe in and out as she washed my back. There was no amount of willpower that could prevent my cock from thickening as I stood naked with the pretty female stroking my skin. I might be Taori, but I was not made of stone. Especially not with the Quaibyn raging deep inside me and fighting for dominion of my soul.

"You should probably turn around so I can clean your chest."

"Hand me the cloth, and I will clean it," I said through gritted teeth, holding my hand back so she could give me the wet fabric.

"You really have a hard time letting someone else be in charge, don't you?"

"Well, I am kalesh of my ship. That means I have overseen my crew for many decades. It is a hard habit to break."

"Wait. I thought your name was Kalesh."

I twisted my head back to meet her gaze. "My name is Naz. My title is Kalesh, but I did not mind you calling me Kalesh."

She gave me an amused look. "So, I was calling you the Taori version of captain? I'll bet you didn't mind that."

"Kalesh means more in our language than captain. The kalesh is like a father to his crew, binding the warriors together like a true family of brothers."

Her eyes grew even wider. "So, I was calling you daddy?"

I fought the urge to smile but lost that battle. "In a manner of speaking."

Her mouth dropped open, and my gaze went instinctively to her full lips. A pang of desire jolted though me, and I closed my hand around the cloth in her hand. There was no way I could control the impending fever if she continued to bathe me. Not when she looked so enticing—and when she called me daddy.

"It's fine," she said, closing her mouth and tugging back on the cloth. "I can finish."

"You should not," I managed to say, as I yanked the cloth from her hand.

With a yelp, Tyrria lost her balance and fell forward into the pool splashing loudly behind me. I spun around and lifted her, spluttering and coughing, so that she stood facing me in the water.

She swiped water from her eyes. "You..."

"I did not mean for you to fall," I said, before her accusations could fly.

She opened her mouth again, but then her gaze dropped to my cock jutting out long and rigid from my body, just below the surface of the water. Even though the water distorted things slightly, it was easy to see the three large crowns running down the length of it.

Tyrria emitted another noise, this one more high-pitched and breathier. I fisted my hands by my side to keep from crushing my mouth to hers and swallowing her feminine sounds.

When the door burst open again, I was grateful for the intrusion as I staggered back.

The guards appraised the situation and gave approving grunts. "It looks like you know how to take care of a fighter after all." Then they frowned at Tyrria. "Get both of you dried and dressed for the battle."

I swung my gaze to the burly aliens. "So soon?" I had expected more time between bouts.

One of the guards grunted. "Both fighters perished in the last fight. We are down one combatant."

Then the entirety of their request hit me. "Both of us?"

"Didn't you know your attendant attends all your fights?"

SUBDUE

I cursed under my breath. Just what I needed—a distraction while I battled to the death.

Tyrria

I PICKED up my pace as I walked behind the Taori and the two guards flanking him. His black hair was swept back, and an errant droplet of water snaked down his bare shoulders as he strode forward without so much as a backward glance. He wore a clean pair of shorts, revealing that the gash on his leg had healed remarkably quickly, and he'd draped the steel mesh sash over one shoulder again. His skin was clean, although the dark marks that covered almost every exposed bit made it hard to know for certain. The only reason I knew was that I'd personally scrubbed almost half of him.

I gulped as I thought about the parts I hadn't scrubbed. Holy righteous gods of the Kayling, I'd never seen a cock like the one the Taori boasted. I could only hope that the water and my eyes had been playing tricks on me and the alien didn't actually have three crowns.

I slowed my step so I wouldn't bump into Naz's swinging tail as it swished behind him in a steady path from one side of the bright hallway to the other. He might appear calm, but I suspected his tail indicated that he was geared up for the upcoming battle. I know the hand nervously fidgeting by my side showed feelings my face never would.

Why hadn't the other females mentioned that I'd be expected to watch the fights? My pulse jangled, and I nervously flicked my fingers through my sideswept bangs that were still damp. It was one thing to know that the Taori would be fighting a battle to the death, but to have to watch it?

I'd never been good with violence or creatures being hurt. As a girl, even a dragonmoth with a broken wing would send me into fits of tears. The idea of watching the Taori who'd vowed to help me escape, being battered in the fighting ring sent waves of nausea through me.

Pull yourself together, Tyrria. You can't let him see that you're scared.

We walked from the high-ceilinged hallways to a more dimly lit corridor, until we were finally in a dank passageway with stone walls that were damp and shiny. I shivered as goose flesh prickled my arms, but I didn't rub them for fear the guards would see me. I refused to let them think I was cold or afraid.

At the end of the dark corridor where the floor was hard-packed dirt, we paused. On the other side of a high, arched opening, bright light illuminated a large, open space. My heart stuttered in my chest when I realized it was the arena where Naz would meet his opponent.

"Where does she go?" The Taori asked, jerking his head back but not looking at me.

"Don't worry about her," one of the guards choked back a gurgling laugh. "She'll be in the box with us." He cut his beady eyes to me. "Not that she'd try to run, with her collar activated."

"Not unless she wants her head blown off," the other guard muttered then laughed at his own joke.

My hand went to the metal ring around my neck, but I forced myself to breathe through the desire to claw at it with my nails.

Naz's shoulders stiffened and his tail stilled, only the dark, furry tip quivering so fast it was vibrating. Then his shoulders

SUBDUE

lowered, and his tail resumed its rhythmic swishing. "She knows better than to run when I'm expecting her to service me after the fight."

The guards laughed so hard their rolls of flesh jiggled, and they cast knowing looks at me. "It looked like she was doing a good job in the pool."

"You shouldn't be thinking about the female." One of the guards said when he'd stopped quivering with laughter. "Not when you're facing a fighter who's won twenty matches in a row."

Naz growled. "What is he?"

"A Zarnock."

Tendrils of fear slithered across my skin and curled sharp talons around my heart. The Zarnock were from an outlaw planet where to survive was to endure one battle to the death after another. They were known to be brutal and without mercy.

"I don't know of them," Naz said.

"Be glad," a guard said, with a shake of his head. "It took a while to capture one of them, but it's paid off. At least, for the director."

"Not for Gorn," the other guard said and spat on the ground.

"Gorn underestimated the Zarnock and got killed for it. But the Zarnock won't last forever. None of them do. The crowds get bored and want fresh blood." He elbowed Naz in the ribs. "That's you."

Before I could warn Naz about how deadly his opponent truly was, the guards were shoving him forward and through the arched entrance. My eyes were blinded by the brilliant sunlight, and I shielded them with one hand as I was bustled to the side and into a box slightly raised above the arena.

I took my seat on a hard, wooden bench, with the two

guards standing post behind me, as Naz strode into the center of the arena. I swung my head from side to side, pausing when I located the other fighters emerging from a far entrance.

My leg jiggled as the Zarnock with blue skin and spikes down his back ran forward, his mouth open in a battle cry so that his pointed teeth were exposed. Even with his tattoos and horns, Naz looked like a Gerrilyn puffen compared to the Zarnock.

I swallowed down a hard lump in my throat and clasped my hands in my lap to keep from wringing them. Was I about to watch the Taori who'd promised to escape with me get torn to pieces?

CHAPTER
EIGHT

Naz

The screams of the crowd rang in my ear, but they didn't drown out the sound of the Zarnock as he ran toward me with his mouth open in a primal scream. His eyes were dark slits, and his blue skin was covered in nubby bumps, but it was his fang-like teeth that made the hair on the back of my neck prickle. They seemed to glimmer in the blistering sunlight, the points catching the rays as the alien barreled toward me.

Unlike my first opponent, this creature appeared to be more beast than humanoid. His long arms brushed the dusty ground as he raced forward and used his bloodied knuckles for balance. If what the guards had said was true, he was a strong enough fighter to take down a series of opponents, although I wondered if it was his fighting skill that helped him prevail, or his combination of teeth, spikes, and speed.

I braced my legs wide, assessing the creature as he drew closer, and the shrieks of the crowd swelled to the point that the ground vibrated, and my own body pulsed with the bloodthirsty roar. Although I didn't take my eyes off my attacker, the crowd was a sea of vicious, red faces and thrusting arms behind him. I didn't know who wanted me dead more—the Zarnock or the spectators.

Once I was within striking range, the Zarnock leapt into the air toward me, his eyes narrowed in malice. I dove forward, using his momentum to put distance between us and hitting the dirt hard before I rolled to my feet. Spinning, I saw that the creature had landed and skidded across the ground, kicking up a cloud of dust as he pivoted back to me.

Now, he was angry. His thin upper lip curled as he eyed me, and I wondered if his other opponents had been killed in his first attack run.

I fisted my hands and squared my shoulders. The creature was intimidating, but I didn't know how clever he was, as a trail of drool dripped from the corner of his mouth.

The crowd's chants hadn't ceased, although they'd groaned when I'd leapt from his reach. It was clear the Xulonians liked their battles bloody, and from the dried flecks of reddish brown and green on the alien's spikes, I had no doubt the Zarnock had obliged them in all his previous fights.

With another chilling cry, the creature lunged for me, his hand reaching for me and the talons scraping the flesh of my arm. I dodged to one side, ducking as he spun high and rotated so that his spikes slashed the air above me. I barely managed to avoid being impaled by the spikes running the length of his spine, and I stumbled forward as I regained my balance.

The Zarnock landed in a crouch, scowling when he saw that his move had failed to injure me. He lifted his head to the sky and released a wail that iced my skin. The Xulonian crowd went wild, as they all replicated his war cry. The red-skinned aliens jumped up and down so violently in the stands that the arena appeared to sway, and the ground trembled.

I stole a quick glance at Tyrria as she sat in the box to the left of the fighters' entrance to the arena. Although the small seating area was walled off from the rest of the crowd, it was only elevated slightly from ground level, so I could see her leg jiggling, and her hands clutched tightly in her lap. Her pretty features were twisted in obvious worry, and I wondered how much violence she'd seen in her life.

I had no idea the average life span for a half Lycithian-half Kayling, but she appeared very young. Even the Taori who appeared younger than me were many decades older than other species who appeared to be the same age. Not only did we age slowly, but our species was long-lived—and I was the eldest on my sky ship. I'd seen more battles than I could count and killed scores of enemies. Blood and battle didn't give me pause, but I suspected the female hadn't lived the long life of a Taori warrior. It was clear from her tormented expression that she'd never watched a battle to the death.

Not that I had any intention of dying. One day, I would answer the seductive whispers of the shadowland, but today was not that day. I had a crew to reunite, a mission to complete, a family legacy to restore, and now an innocent female to save.

Thoughts of Tyrria standing in front of me in the pool rushed to my mind. She'd looked shocked when she'd seen my hard cock, but then her eyes had flashed with something I hadn't seen in a long time—desire. The hunger in her gaze had been undeniable as her pupils had darkened and she'd bitten her plump bottom lip. If the guards hadn't walked in at that moment...

"Kalesh!" A high-pitched shriek tore through the air and snapped my thoughts back to reality.

I didn't need to turn to know that it was Tyrria's voice warning me as the Zarnock slammed into me, knocking me to the ground. With a roar, he flipped onto his back with lightning-fast speed. I jerked myself just as quickly to the side as his spikes drove into the ground, but one of them pierced the fleshy part of my bicep.

Leaping to my feet, I slapped a hand over my bleeding arm and backed away from the alien, who was already up and ambling toward me. I muttered a curse under my breath as my arm throbbed and blood seeped through my fingers. The wound was superficial, but now that the creature had drawn blood, he looked manic.

Fool, I thought. *You let yourself get distracted by the female.*

This was why there were no females on Taori ships, and why I'd avoided entanglements with anyone but the occasional pleasurer. Females made warriors lose their focus, and losing focus meant death. I dropped my hand, ignoring the blood dripping down my arm and onto the dusty arena floor. I needed to forget about Tyrria if I wanted to stay alive.

I gritted my teeth and faced down the Zarnock again. It was time to show the creature what it meant to fight a kalesh of the Taori.

Then another scream pierced the air.

CHAPTER NINE

Tyrria

My heart lurched when the Zarnock impaled one of his spikes into Naz's arm, and I gasped and smacked a hand over my mouth when I saw the blood oozing between his fingers. Even though his bicep was heavily tattooed, the gash had looked deep and ugly.

Why had the Taori lost his concentration? I pressed my lips together so hard they hurt. If I hadn't screamed at him, he might have been completely gored by the alien. A wave of nausea swept over me as I imagined Naz lying dead in the middle of the arena.

Why did the idea of him being hurt or killed affect me so? I barely knew the warrior, and I knew better than to put my faith in any male. I frowned at my own cynicism. There was something about the Taori that made me want to trust him more than I'd wanted anything in a long time. I didn't know if it was the strange way he talked, or the certainty of his voice when he'd promised to save me, but I couldn't brush him aside so easily.

It would have been easier if I could have, I thought, as I watched him standing in the arena with his blood splattering on the dirt at his feet. Caring for a virtual stranger was the last thing I needed in my life, but for some inexplicable reason, I found myself caring a lot about what happened to the Taori captain.

Not only did I believe he was a decent alien who cared deeply for his crew, he was convinced he was going to get off the battle moon. His confidence gave me confidence, especially since he'd vowed to take me with him. Not only that, I hated the thought of starting over with a new fighter, and I had a feeling they all weren't as easy as Naz.

I eyed the Zarnock. The thought of attending to a creature like him who was truly one step above a mindless killing machine sent cold fingers of fear sliding down my spine. I tore my gaze from him, telling myself that Naz would win, even though my stomach churned at the traitorous thought that he might not.

Unease stirred within me as I remembered the Taori catching my eye before he'd been injured. His hesitation hadn't been more than a few seconds, but it had been enough to give the Zarnock an advantage.

I was the reason he'd been wounded.

There was no doubt that I'd stirred something in him when we were in the bathing pool. His rigid cock had been proof of that, but I'd assumed that was because he was naked, and I was so close to him in the water. Then I remembered his reaction when I'd touched him to remove his metal sash. He'd lost all control then, but quickly regained it. I might not be physically close to him now, but my presence might still be a distraction.

I stood, instantly sure of what I needed to do.

"Sit down," one of the guards behind me said.

I turned and shook my head. "I need to leave."

He flicked a bored gaze at me. "Not until the fight is over, and we see if you go back to tend the beast, or if you get someone new."

I bristled at them calling Naz a beast. It was rich if you considered the creature he was currently fighting.

"I can't be here," I said, keeping my voice calm but firm. "I'm distracting him."

"Who?" The other guard asked.

My heart pounded as I slid my gaze to him. "I think I'm the reason he got hurt. I need to leave so I won't distract him again."

The guard's fleshy face contorted before he let loose a belly laugh that made his entire body shake. "You think the beast is going to lose his fight because he's distracted by his female attendant?"

I bit the inside of my lip to keep from snapping back, but I could feel the argument going sideways. "I don't need to be here. Why don't you let me go? I can prepare for when he returns to the room. I'll need to be ready to tend to his wound."

The first guard cocked his head at me. "You're very concerned about a beast you were just assigned to serve."

"I don't want to be the reason he gets hurt," I said through tight teeth. "That's all."

"Admirable," the other guard said, "but you aren't leaving."

I cast a glance back at the arena as the crowd's chants for blood grew louder and more desperate. "I need to get out of this box."

The first guard cut a look to his colleague and shrugged. "You want out? We can let you out."

I released a sigh. Being firm and standing my ground had actually worked. Before I could give myself more than a mental pat on the back, the guard advanced on me, lifted me up by the shoulders and dropped me into the arena.

I screamed as I landed hard on the ground, scrambling to my feet, and trying to climb back into the spectator box.

"You wanted out," the second guard said, joining his colleague to block my way. "Now you get to see how much of a distraction you really are—and if your fighter is good enough to save both of you."

I spun around at the same moment the Zarnock's face swung to me, and his slitted eyes flared. This was very bad.

CHAPTER TEN

Naz

I jerked my head to follow the scream, but my eyes couldn't compute what I saw. Why was Tyrria in the arena? Then my gaze slid to the two tusked guards standing above her, their hands braced on their hips and their expressions both amused and malicious. They were the reason she was in the arena with me. They'd thrown her in, or they refused to let her out. Either way, they were the reason she was now in danger.

My fingers tingled as I curled my hands into fists, mentally adding the guards to the list of creatures I would kill when I had the chance. My list was getting long.

The Zarnock swung his head to Tyrria, and his body stilled. He lifted his nose into the air and breathed in before opening his mouth to expose his rows of spiky teeth.

I didn't wait for him to let out his bloodcurdling scream

and start charging her. Instead, I barreled toward Tyrria, ignoring the look of terror on her face or the fact that I didn't know what I was going to do once I reached her. I couldn't throw her back into the spectator box. The guards would only throw her back out. I couldn't toss her into the stands. I had the sinking feeling that the Xulonians who had enough blood lust to enjoy the battle moon wouldn't hesitate to return Tyrria to the ring or tear her apart themselves.

My only option was to shield her from the Zarnock until I could kill him. But that was easier said than done.

"It doesn't matter," I muttered darkly as I ran. "Our meeting was written in the stars. This day is not the day either of us answers the whispers of the shadowland."

When I reached Tyrria, I skidded to a stop and kicked up a cloud of dust around both of us. "Stay behind me."

"Fine by me," she said, her gaze darting over my shoulder and her eyes growing wide.

I whirled around just in time to see the alien's row of spikes glint in the sunlight as they flew toward me. I pulled Tyrria down and to the side until we bumped up against the barrier, curling my body over hers to shield her from the vicious spikes that were as sharp as blades. The hair by my ear rustled as one of the spikes came so close a tuft of black was sheared off and floated down to the ground.

I didn't want to see what else might be sliced off next, so I grabbed Tyrria's hand and pulled her with me as I ran toward the center of the ring. There might not be any protection out there, but at least the Zarnock couldn't pin us against a barrier.

The roar of the crowd was deafening. The sick creatures were screaming even louder than they had been before. They weren't horrified that a female was in the ring with me, running for her life—they loved it.

I grunted in disgust. More to add to my list of creatures to

SUBDUE

punish. It was a good thing I would be reuniting my crew. I would need every last Taori to help me exact my punishment on the Xulonians.

"What's the plan?" Tyrria asked between ragged breaths.

I still clasped her hand tightly, although her delicate, soft hand was completely enveloped by my larger, calloused one. I readjusted my grip but didn't release it.

My mind raced, as I watched the Zarnock rise to his feet and pin his gaze on us from across the expanse of the arena. I'd been a kalesh of the Taori for most of my life now, but the wars I'd fought had been on battlefields teeming with Taori warriors and enemy combatants. Blood had flowed freely, and bodies had littered the ground as we'd triumphed over our enemies again and again. But this was an entirely different kind of fight.

As much experience as I'd had in the battle ring on our sky ship, I'd never fought a creature like the Zarnock, and I'd never done it while trying to protect a frail female. I gulped down the sharp taste of fear as my brain whirred with battle strategy, and I rejected almost every one of them.

"Kalesh?" Tyrria squeezed my hand. "Naz?"

I glanced down at her. She'd asked me about my plan, but I still wasn't sure I had a foolproof one. "Avoid the spikes and teeth."

She raised a brow as she swept her pink hair off her forehead, smudging some dirt on her face as she did. "Good tip. Thanks."

I recognized her snarky tone but didn't have time to reply before the Zarnock was screaming and running toward us. The roar of the crowd rose as he drew closer, and I lowered myself into a battle crouch and tucked Tyrria behind me. "Into the valley of death ride the Ten Thousand."

Before I could whisper the last part of the mantra, the alien was flying through the air. I sidestepped, pushing Tyrria even farther away, then I reached up and snatched one of the creature's spikes. Pain shot through my hand as I closed my fingers around the sharp edge, but I gritted my teeth as I yanked him hard to the ground then released him and backed away.

The alien yelped in agony as his head hit the dirt, and his body crumpled. The cheers of the spectators died for a beat, before they swelled again in cheers, this time for me.

"Bloodthirsty and fickle," I muttered, casting a dark look at the stands and the open-mouthed, crimson faces contorted in sick pleasure.

The moment I took to steal a glance at the audience was too long, as a scream made me drag my gaze back to the Zarnock, who'd risen from the ground and snatched Tyrria by the arm. My heart seemed to stop as he jerked her flush to him, but he didn't impale her on his talon-like fingernails or snap her neck. Instead, he ran his nose up the side of her neck as he inhaled.

He was scenting the female. My female, I thought, as a possessive growl escaped from my lips.

Fire suffused my body as I watched the alien curl one hand around to cup her breast, his mouth curving up in a poisonous smile as he started to tear at her clothes. Then there was no sound but the hammering of my heart and the rushing of blood in my ears, as the red haze consumed me.

Tyrria

My own breathing had stopped as the blue-skinned alien held me. I was facing Naz, but he was too far away to reach me before the Zarnock could snap my neck. I knew this because the creature's cold fingers were coiled around my hairline, and his knife-edged fingernails teased my throat.

The aliens in the stands were jumping up and down at the turn of events, their hysteria making the ground rumble and bile rise in my gut. I pressed my lips together to keep the sharp tang down, my eyes locking on the Taori. The only one who could save me was him, and I hated that.

How had I gotten myself in a situation where I had to rely on a male to survive. Not only that, a male I barely knew. Even the males I'd known for ages hadn't protected me, but now my life was in this Taori's hands.

As his iridescent-blue eyes held mine, a calm settled over me. He didn't look scared or worried. He seemed determined, and his certainty made me believe that he would save me— even from a terrifying creature like the Zarnock.

The cold-skinned alien dragged his nose up the side of my neck, inhaling the whole time, and a shiver of revulsion shook me. It hit me that the creature might not want to kill me, but that didn't make me feel any better. The alternative that his icy hand on my breast confirmed was not an improvement over decapitation.

I recoiled as the Zarnock's hands started tearing at my clothes as if he was possessed. An involuntary shriek left me as I crossed my hands over myself. No way was I going to be stripped naked in the middle of a packed arena without putting up a fight.

My cry was drowned by a roar of fury that made the Zarnock freeze. Then Naz was on him, and it was the Taori who looked possessed. His blue eyes had gone entirely black and there was none of the calm resolve in them I'd seen earlier. There was only rage and madness.

For a moment, I wasn't sure if he was my savior, or the alien I should fear. He grabbed the Zarnock by the spikes, oblivious to razor-like edges slicing into his hands and flung the alien to the ground. Instead of pausing, he then leapt on the creature, wrenching off one of the spikes from his back.

The Zarnock shrieked in pain, but Naz didn't even blink as he used the spike to stab the creature. Black blood spurted from the bumpy, blue skin and the screams became more tortured, but the Taori only rammed the spike faster into the flailing body.

I backed away as the Zarnock attempted to get away from Naz, but the Taori's mania seemed to have given him strength that easily overpowered the creature. Even though the Zarnock was bigger, Naz held him down as he struck him in a frenzy. His long tail swished quickly behind him, matching the beat of each thrust.

The Xulonian crowd had gone quiet as more thick, black blood pumped from the alien who'd been their victor for many fights. His body jerked as he was drained of life, but Naz didn't stop, Finally, when there was no sound but the last gurgling gasps from the Zarnock, Naz took the spike and dragged it across his opponent's throat so hard that his head was almost completely severed.

He dropped the spike on the blood-spattered dirt and stood with his chest heaving and his shoulders hunched as he stared down at creature he'd defeated. The Zarnock blood on his body blended in with the dark ink that already covered his skin. Only the specks of black on his silvery-striped horns revealed the evidence of his attack.

I attempted to pull my tattered clothes back onto my body as shocked murmurs passed through the spectators. Then the Taori tipped his head back and emitted a booming cry that reverberated into my bones. In response, the crowd erupted in screams and cheers. They'd clearly decided to embrace their

SUBDUE

new victor, and the air in the arena vibrated with the ear-splitting cheering.

My knees were wobbly, but I managed to walk to Naz, putting a hand gently on his arm. "Thank you."

When he swung his head to meet my gaze, I stumbled back. His eyes were still all pupil, the black cores seeming to burn from within. He raked a primal gaze down my body, making no effort to hide the wanton hunger in his eyes. "Mine."

My pulse jackknifed as I realized the frenzy that had made him such an effective killer had not faded. He looked at me like a predator eyed prey he was about to devour.

Without another word, he picked me up and threw me over his shoulder, striding from the arena to even louder cheers of approval. Even the two guards who'd thrown me into the ring didn't stop him as Naz stalked down the corridor to his quarters. Several female attendants scurried out of the way, shrank to the side, and gaped as we passed, but no one stopped him.

I didn't even make a sound until we were inside the room and the door slammed behind us. He dropped me on the circular bed and loomed over me, his arms braced on each side of me and pinning me in. He let out another growl, as the heat rolled off his body as if he'd been engulfed in flames.

This wasn't the Taori who'd promised to protect me, I thought. This was someone else entirely, and I wanted to know who.

So, I slapped him as hard as I could across the face.

CHAPTER
ELEVEN

~

"Explain to me again how that happened." The Xulonian director walked slowly across the floor, his bony, red fingers poking from the belled sleeves of his beige robe and steepling.

His office was as light-filled and high-ceilinged as the other suites in the upper level of the arena complex, but it didn't have a domed ceiling, or any windows with colored glass. Instead, it was spartan and furnished only with the barest of items—a nearly empty desk, and one chair with a tall back. There was no chair for a visitor, because he didn't welcome intrusion or wish for anyone to be comfortable in his presence.

The hulking guard stood awkwardly as the director paced, his lower lip quivering below his thick, yellowed tusks. "The Zarnock losing?"

The director of the Moorla moon stopped walking a slow circle across the office and pivoted to face the guard. "No." His word was as sharp as ice and just as cold. "The female attendant ending up in the battle arena. We do not bring the creatures here to be fighters. We gather them to attend to the aliens we do recruit to do battle."

The guard shuffled his feet and dropped his gaze to the floor. "It was accidental."

The Xulonian rapped the toe of one shoe on the polished floor. "I understand two guards put her in the arena—on purpose."

"She was trying to leave the fight. She claimed she was distracting her fighter."

The director peered from beneath his hood, tilting his head and eyeing the rotund guard with unmasked disdain. "So, your guards felt the best course of action would be to put her in the fight?"

The guard lifted his head. "The crowd loved it."

"Did they?"

"You should have heard the screams."

The director glided behind a wide desk that matched the pale sand color of the floors and leaned his spindly fingers on the surface. "If I wanted to hear the primitive screams of our citizens starving for some excitement in their bland lives, I would go to the arena myself."

The guard frowned and dipped his head again.

"There's one way to know if what you say is true." The red-skinned alien snatched a flat device from the desk and tapped his fingers on the surface. He scowled at the numbers, swiped the shiny surface, and then hummed to himself. "The signups for the beast's next match are unusually high, but that could be because of the brutal way he dispatched the Zarnock."

The director might not attend the match in person, but he did watch the highlights. After all, it was his job to oversee the battle moon and ensure that each dimensional in the arena was inhabited. The more cheering, paying citizens filling the stands, the more money for him and the Collective that controlled the planet Xulon.

"Or it might be because your kind liked seeing the alien go primal to defend the female," the guard said. "If you'd heard the arena shake when he threw her over his shoulder and carried her out, you'd know it wasn't just about the killing."

The director put the device back on his desk. "Are we sure the female was unharmed when he took her? It's getting harder to replace the attendants with fresh females. Your Hettite brothers have been shirking in their duty to find us more females. Something about ships getting wise to their tricks." He waved a hand dismissively. "That doesn't matter. What does matter is keeping the females we do have."

"But what if one of them can make you so much it doesn't matter if you need to get more?"

The director pushed back his hood. "Are you suggesting we repeat your guards' blunder?"

The head guard recoiled slightly at the sight of the scarlet skin pulled tight over the angular lines of the alien's skull. "The beast won't let her get hurt. I've never seen any creature go as berserk as he did when the Zarnock touched her."

"Are you willing to bet her life on it?" The Xulonian gave him an evil smile. "Are you willing to bet yours?"

The guard stammered something unintelligible as the director gave a dry, mirthless chuckle. "We'll try it for the next fight and see if you're right." He narrowed his black eyes. "For your sake, I hope you are." He waved a hand toward the door. "Now go, and make sure the beast isn't mauling his attendant like he did the Zarnock."

The guard bowed as he backed from the room, muttering to himself. "He might be mauling her, but not like he did the Zarnock." He let a guttural laugh jiggle his gut. He'd seen the look in the beast's eyes before, and he knew exactly what the alien wanted from the pink-haired female.

He trod slowly down the hallway. He wasn't in any rush to interrupt the creature. Let the beast have his fill of her. After the show he'd put on, he deserved to bury himself in a female.

CHAPTER
TWELVE

Naz

My cheek stung as I held my hand to it. I shook my head to clear the fog in my brain, blinking rapidly as I realized I was looking down at Tyrria. Her eyes were wide as she stared up at me and one of her palms was flushed pink.

"Did you hit me?" I asked, my own voice sounding hoarse to my ears.

She didn't answer immediately, her gaze studying me and her eyebrows knitting together. "Are you back?"

I realized that my chest was heaving as I hovered over her. I straightened, wondering why she was on the bed and how we'd both gotten back to my quarters. "Back?"

Tyrria scooted away until her back bumped the headboard. "You went to a dark place. At least, that's what it seemed like."

I rubbed a hand to my temple, before noticing a consider-

SUBDUE

able amount of thick, black goo on my hands, which were lacerated and dripping with my own blood, as well. Where did the black substance come from? I dropped my gaze to my body where more black streaked my flesh, although it didn't stand out against my markings like the green blood had.

My shoulder twinged as I moved my arm, and I saw that I'd been injured there. Now, *that* I remembered. The Zarnock had impaled me with one of the spikes running the length of his spine. I could recall the sharp pain that had been replaced by a dull thud as blood oozed from the gash.

I remembered being stabbed by my enemy, but I had no memory of how I'd gotten covered in black, putrid-smelling goo. All I knew for sure was that I needed to rid myself of the smell and feel of the slick black substance.

Staggering to the sunken pool, I jumped in and sank to the bottom. My sliced hands and cut shoulder instantly burned from the heat, but the rest of my body welcomed the shocking temperature. I stood and let the water stream from my skin and take the black goo with it. Instead of pooling on the surface, the black melted away along with the foul scent that was overpowered by the spicy perfume of the pool. The sting of the heat gave way to an almost pleasurable tingling sensation around my wounds, and I wondered if the water contained healing properties. It hadn't been lost on me that the cut in my leg from the first fight had healed quickly after a dunk in the pool, but I'd brushed it off, thinking the cut hadn't been as deep as I'd imagined. But what if I'd been wrong? It would make sense in a fighter's suite since the faster we healed, the faster we could battle again.

When I was sure I'd scrubbed every bit of the goo off, I hopped out and raked my fingers over my face and down my dripping wet hair. They brushed my horns, and I was glad to feel that they were also clean.

Despite the heat of the water, my skin no longer sizzled like it was on fire, and my heart had regained its steady rhythm. Glancing at my hands, I saw that the cuts were knitting together, proving right my theory about the water. I was in wet shorts, but at least I was clean, and my mind wasn't muddled. I snatched a towel from a rack on the wall and wrapped it around my waist then pulled off my shorts from underneath it.

"Better?"

I glanced at Tyrria who was still on the bed, although she'd slid to the edge, so her legs were hanging off. "What was the black substance?"

She wrinkled her nose. "That was the Zarnock's blood."

I'd suspected as much, but it was still confronting to hear her confirm it. "The creature is dead?"

"Very." Then she cocked her head at me. "You don't remember killing him?"

My breath hitched in my chest. I'd killed the Zarnock? I scoured my brain to pull up any memories of that, but there was nothing but a red haze of rage like a blanket over my mind. I gave a curt shake of my head, as I walked to the table of food and poured myself a goblet of alien wine.

I downed the drink in a single gulp and turned to Tyrria. "How did I do it?"

She made another face. "You broke off one of the spikes on his back and stabbed him with it. Then when he was immobilized, you used it to slit his throat. Decapitate him, really."

The wine threatened to come back up, but I forced the sour liquid to stay down as I glanced at the cuts in my hands that had stopped bleeding. There was no reason why I should let this one death bother me. I'd dispatched hundreds of my enemy—some in hand-to-hand combat and some with photon weapons from my sky ship. This was no different. The

Zarnock had tried to kill me. It had been him or me. I'd done what I had to do.

It wasn't the killing that bothered me. It was the fact that I had no recollection of it. From the way Tyrria described it—even though I knew she was holding back on her description—I'd killed the Zarnock in a frenzy. The only time I'd ever acted in such a wild and uncontrolled manner had been when I'd been in the complete throes of the Quaibyn.

Unlike most of my Taori brothers who experienced the Quaibyn as a slowing approaching compulsion that grew stronger bit by bit, the fever struck me fast and hard. When I was consumed by the curse of my people, I lost all awareness of my actions and memory of them afterward. The bouts had never lasted long, and they'd always been frenzies of lust that the Quaibyn priestesses or pleasurers had reported as just enthusiastic and dominant sex, but they'd all said what Tyrria had—that I'd gone to a different place or become a different Taori.

The sick feeling swirled in my gut as I focused on Tyrria again, and for the first time I worried that I'd done something to her. She appeared fine, but I was also pretty sure she'd hit me. "Did I harm you?"

"I'm fine." She stood from the bed and walked toward me. "Thanks to you, actually. You only killed the Zarnock after he threatened me."

My pulse spiked. "Did *he* hurt you?"

She gave a weak smile. "No, but he scared me." She motioned with one hand to her ripped clothes. "And he ruined my outfit."

I shifted my gaze to her body and my anger flared fresh. Her garments were dirty and torn, a strap of white fabric barely holding one side of her shirt on her shoulder. "Then he deserved his punishment."

"I'd say he got what was coming to him."

I flicked my eyes to the bathing pool. "You should also rid yourself of the reminders of the battle."

She let her gaze dart to the steaming water. "Soon enough." She joined me at the table and poured herself a goblet of wine, then refilled my glass. "I have no problem with what you did to protect me and to take out the Zarnock, but do you mind telling me what happened out there?"

"I don't know."

She scrunched her lips to one side and gave me a skeptical look.

"I truly do not know what happened because I have no memory," I told her, my hand curling around the goblet and holding it tight. "This has happened to me before, but I didn't think it would strike me again so soon. Until we were pulled through the temporal wormhole, I had many astro-years to go before I would have worried about the Quaibyn."

Tyrria brushed her fingers through her bangs to push them off her forehead, a motion I noticed she did often when she was nervous. "The Quaibyn? Who are they?"

I grinned briefly, despite the seriousness of the situation. "The Quaibyn is not an alien species. It is a curse on my people."

"You're going to have to be more specific than that."

"All Taori males are afflicted with the Quaibyn once they reach maturity. It only hits us once every decade and has historically been easy to manage. On my home world, we have Quaibyn priestesses, and even when we travel across galaxies we have been able to plan our trips and stops accordingly."

"So, you have this Quaibyn, and it makes you forget things?"

"Yes and no. I believe I am experiencing the early stages of the Quaibyn, but it doesn't cause me to forget things. It consumes me, and when I'm deep in its throes, I remember nothing. I am acting on pure primal instinct."

She nodded slowly, as if she was slowly grasping what I was saying. "So out there in the arena, you did everything without being conscious of it?" Her mouth fell open. "The Quaibyn turns you into a killing machine?"

I shook my head. "Not a killing machine. Everything I did in the arena would have been to protect you—the female under my protection. If I killed, it was to defend you."

"Then the Quaibyn is...?"

"The most powerful mating fever you've ever seen."

CHAPTER THIRTEEN

Tyrria

I took a huge gulp of my wine, draining the glass and setting the empty goblet on the table. Maybe I'd heard him wrong. Mating fever wasn't actually a thing for an alien as advanced as his species appeared to be, was it? I flicked my hand across my bangs, feathering the hair out of my face. "Did you say mating fever?"

The Taori met my gaze for a beat then wrenched his eyes away. "It is a curse upon my kind. One that has afflicted us for as long as anyone can remember, but it's something we are used to and can plan around."

I lifted my eyebrows at this. The idea of planning around an all-consuming fever that sent you into a murderous rage seemed almost comical, but I couldn't laugh. Not when I'd seen how possessed Naz had been, and how genuinely unaware he was of what had happened in the arena. "So, it was a mating frenzy that made you kill the Zarnock?"

He gave a brusque shake of his head. "That wasn't a mating frenzy. The fever hasn't advanced that far. Not yet. What you witnessed was my reaction to you being threatened."

"So, your mating fever also fires up your defensive instincts?"

He darted a brief gaze to me. "When it comes to a female I've sworn to protect, yes."

I gulped, wondering if he regretted making a promise to help me, and wondering if there was more to the vow than I understood. "It must be awful to have an illness that robs you of your willpower and your memory."

Naz laughed, the sound carrying an edge of bitterness. "Not all Taori experience the same loss of memory that I do. My complete shift in personality is unique to my fever, which is why it's crucial I escape from this battle moon. Time is not on my side."

"What about a cure?" I asked. "If your species has dealt with this for so long, surely they've developed a cure or ways to slow its progression."

"The only way to slow the progress is sedation, which is not an option for me here." He strode away from me and leaned his hands on the empty dining table. "Otherwise, the cure for mating fever is exactly what you would expect."

The gears in my brain turned, the answer clicking into place as my pulse quickened. "Oh."

Naz twisted his neck, his smile strained. "I would like to assure you that I would never lay a hand on you, but I don't know if I can make that promise. I have never been pushed past the brink of my fever consuming me without release. I want to believe that my Taori honor is so deeply ingrained that I would never dishonor a female, but the Quaibyn takes over my body. I don't remember brutally murdering my opponent in the arena just now. How can I expect that I would remember myself when my body is starved for a mate to quench my fever?"

My mouth went dry. I liked the Taori. I even found myself attracted to him. My body reacted to him like it never had before. That didn't mean I was up for being the female who would quench his mating lust. If it was anything like the blood lust I'd just witnessed in the battle ring, there was no guarantee I'd survive curing him of his fever.

"What happens if you don't find a mate for your fever?"

His shoulders stiffened and his brows pressed together. "If the Quaibyn isn't cured, I will go mad."

"Mad like you went in the arena?"

He chuckled mirthlessly. "That was a temporary blood rage. Madness brought on by the Quaibyn is true insanity that leads to death." He lowered his voice to an almost intelligible growl. "And then worse."

Goose bumps prickled angrily across my arms. Worse? What was worse than death? I didn't want to ask, because I didn't know how many more hard truths I was up for at the moment.

Not only did we have to escape so he wouldn't be killed in the arena, and I wouldn't be assigned to another—possibly more dangerous and demanding—fighter, but now I knew we needed to get off the battle moon before Naz's mating fever took over. I might not have known the alien warrior for long, but he'd already saved my life once. I couldn't let him go mad if I could help it. As long as helping him didn't entail becoming his unwilling mate. I might be half Lycithian, but that didn't mean I was anyone's whore.

"I thought I'd had a shit time of it lately, but you win," I finally said with a heavy sigh. "This is not great."

"You have a talent for understatement, female."

I ignored his comment as I walked over to the table and pulled out one of the high-backed chairs. I flopped into it. "So, we need to make sure you win all your fights until we can figure out a way to escape. Then we need to find the rest of your crew and reunite you all so you can return to your mission."

"You forgot that we need to rain vengeance on the Xulonians for destroying my ship, kidnapping innocent aliens, and tormenting others for their amusement."

"Right." I held up three fingers before flipping up a fourth. "And along the way we need to cure you of your mating fever."

Naz grunted, tightening his grip on the chair back until his knuckles went white. "I will be fine. We should focus on the rest."

If his reaction in the arena had been any indication, I doubted that he would be fine, but I wasn't going to argue with him.

The door opened behind us, and a guard entered that I didn't recognize. It wasn't one of the ones who'd escorted us to the arena and tossed me into the battle ring, which was probably a good thing. The Taori might be the one with the blood rage, but I wasn't exactly in a forgive-and-forget mood when it came to the tusked creatures who seemed to revel in their captives' torment.

The creature's dark, beady eyes lingered on Naz before flitting to me. "You both look recovered from the fight."

Kalesh Naz straightened and turned, crossing his thick arms over his chest. The guards might be huge, and armed with electrified batons, but they'd also seen the Taori go berserk against an alien many times deadlier than them.

The guard stepped back and held his baton across his body as if it was a shield. Then he cleared his throat. "Since you defeated the reigning champion, you won't be required to fight again until tomorrow."

"How generous," I said, not bothering to hide the snark in my voice.

The creature narrowed his gaze at me. "You should rest, too, female."

"Don't worry about me. I don't plan to get myself thrown into the ring again." Now that I knew the Taori was fierce enough to kill a Zarnock, I wouldn't be worried about being a distraction.

The guard smiled through his yellowed tusks. "You won't be thrown in, but you will be joining the beast for all his fights."

"What?" Naz dropped his arms, his fists tight.

The guard raised his baton slightly. "The director decided. The viewer reaction to you and the female was too overwhelming to ignore. From now on, you fight together."

Naz glanced at me, his face tight with barely controlled fury. "She is not a fighter. I'm the one you want. I will kill for you. Leave her out of it."

The guard shook his head and his jowls quivered. "What the director says goes."

The Taori growled, causing my hair to stand on end and the alien guard to back hurriedly from the room.

"One more creature to add to my list of those I will kill before this is over," he said in a velvety hum that vibrated with menace.

I believed him. As impossible as it was to think that the Taori captive would do what he said he would do—escape, reunite his crew, punish the Xulonians—his certainty gave me no doubt he would do it all.

I drew in a breath and turned to him. "If I'm going to be in the arena with you, I need to know how to fight. You need to teach me."

His blue eyes flared with disbelief and then he nodded. "You cannot learn to be a skilled fighter in so short a time, but I can teach you to defend yourself."

"Good. Let's do it." What I didn't say aloud was that I wanted to learn to fight because I was afraid there would be a time in the very near future when I might need to defend myself from the kalesh himself. At this point, I truly didn't know who the more dangerous threat to me was—the violent creatures I'd be meeting in the arena or the Taori with mating fever who faced me.

CHAPTER FOURTEEN

Naz

"Again!" Tyrria sucked in a breath as a bead of sweat trickled down the side of her face. She swiped at her hair, slicking it to the side even though it would only flop back as soon as we resumed fighting.

We'd been at it since waking, although I couldn't complain after the restorative sleep that made me feel like a new Taori. We'd both collapsed with exhaustion after our first long and arduous day in the battle ring—and after I'd made my confession. Even the Quiabyn hadn't interfered with my hunger for sleep, as we'd passed the night on the huge bed without so much as touching, but Tyrria had insisted on starting her training as soon as we were both awake. I hadn't argued. I was grateful to have a distraction, even if the sight of her flushed skin didn't do much to staunch my mating fever.

I adjusted the sash across my chest, the jangling of the cool metal muffled by my long-sleeved shirt. I'd requested clothing beyond the barely-there battle shorts that I was required to wear in the arena, and the guards had begrudgingly complied. After all, I was their newest victor and the reason their arena was packed with cheering, red-skinned aliens, so I suspected they'd been instructed to keep me happy. As happy as a prisoner could be.

I shoved one of the sleeves of my shirt up my forearm then frowned and pushed it down, reminding myself why I wanted to be so covered as the female lunged for me. Her hands reached for my arm, but I deftly pivoted and spun around, coiling an arm around her waist and rotating her so she was facing away from me, and my other arm was snug under her chin.

She huffed out an irritated breath. "No fair. You're bigger and stronger."

I released my grip on her and backed away, glad that the garments that covered my skin and made me sweat prevented my skin from making contact with hers. "Strength has nothing to do with it."

She cocked an eyebrow at me and gave me a pointed up and down glance. "It helps."

I grinned at her, raising one shoulder in tacit admission. "It might help."

Tyrria bent over at the waist and braced her hands on her knees. "I don't understand how this is going to help when we're in the arena. I'm still half your size and probably half the size of every opponent we'll meet."

Her face was flushed from exertion and her eyes sparkled, and I had to fight not to wonder if this was what she looked like when she was in the throes of passion. Even the sweat glistening her skin made a low simmer of desire rumble in my core.

I closed my eyes for a beat and forced myself to think about something else—anything else—so my mating fever wouldn't be stoked. I thought of the steel interior of our sky ship and the ever-present smell of warriors. There was little less appealing than the ripe smell of hundreds of Taori males living and working on top of each other.

"Naz?"

I opened my eyes, returning instantly to the light-filled and more fragrant quarters in the alien battle complex. Tyrria stood across from me with her hands in loose fists and her knees bent in a fighting stance.

"Winning battles isn't about size or might," I said, the heat in my gut cooled enough for me to proceed. "It's about strategy. Even a smaller warrior can outthink his opponent and win."

"So, what's our strategy?"

I thought about that for a moment. I'd been focused on teaching Tyrria basic grappling techniques, but she was right. That would only take her so far if our opponents were all larger and trained in fighting. There wasn't enough time for me to teach her to be a proficient warrior, and even if there was, I didn't want her engaged in hand-to-hand combat in the battle ring. The Xulonians craved blood, so the fights were vicious. Not the best way for an inexperienced fighter to learn.

"We have an advantage our opponents won't." I spun and strode toward the table that had earlier held food, and which now only held carafes of wine and water.

I poured myself a goblet of water and drained it in a single gulp. The cold drink served to dampen my inner fire even more, and my heart rate slowed to a steady thump. I filled another goblet and turned back to Tyrria, extending my arm.

She walked toward me and took the goblet. "I'm on pins and needles."

I flicked my gaze to the floor, my brow creasing in confusion. Where were the pins and needles?

"It's an expression," she said with a giggle. "I heard it from some human traders who came to Kayling. It means I'm eager to hear about our tactical advantage."

I had limited experience with humans, but I was not surprised that their language made no sense. From what the Drexians had told us, they were a species still developing basic space travel, although perhaps in five hundred years they'd made progress. They'd apparently made it to Kayling, wherever that was.

I poured myself more water. "There are two of us."

Tyrria took a sip and didn't respond right away. "That's it? That's our big advantage? But one of the two of us can't fight worth a damn."

"Irrelevant. You are the distraction."

She narrowed her eyes at me. "You mean I'm the bait?"

It took me a moment to process the word. "A sacrifice to be devoured? No. There is no scenario in which you would be eaten."

"Good to know," she muttered from behind the rim of the chunky, glass goblet.

"Unless our opponents are accustomed to fighting groups, they will be expecting a single attacker. We will surprise them by coming from two different directions, and you will appear to be the more erratic enemy. Your fighting style and appearance will naturally draw their attention while I will attack by stealth."

Tyrria lowered her glass and drummed her fingers on it as she held it with both hands. "I don't know whether to be flattered or offended. Am I drawing their attention because I'm so striking, or because I appear ridiculous?"

"Does it need to be one or the other?"

This didn't make her smile. "Why don't you explain exactly what you want me to do to get the fighters to pay attention to me and not you?"

I thought about this and the best way to phrase it. I wasn't used to half Lycithian-half Kayling females, but I already got the idea they were more sensitive than those on Taor. "You will already attract the gaze of any male with your feminine beauty and with the surprising presence of a female in the arena. This will catch any fighter off-guard."

She nodded as if acknowledging this, but still her eyes were narrowed in suspicion. "You don't have to say that, you know."

Now I was confused. "Say what?"

"That I'm beautiful. I know I look too much like a Lycithian to be pretty."

I stared at her. By any measure of feminine allure, she was beautiful, and her pink hair and silver eyes only made her more appealing. "If you look Lycithian, then that species must have beautiful females."

Her cheeks flushed. "Not to the Kayling."

"Then the Kayling are fools," I growled, feeling a flash of protectiveness swell in my chest. "If you wish, I can add them to the list of those I am enacting vengeance on once we escape."

A sly smile spilt her face. "No need to punish them on my account. Besides, I'm glad the Kayling males didn't find me attractive because they weren't my type."

The thought of Tyrria having a type of male she preferred made my nerves jangle. What were the chances she preferred horns, a tail, and silvered hair?

"I'm guessing there's more to your strategy than just me distracting the other fighters with my presence," she said, pulling my thoughts away from my fresh worry and back to my plan.

SUBDUE

I cleared my throat. "Once you have gained their attention then you will keep it focused on you with your erratic actions."

She placed her goblet on the table and folded her arms across her chest. "Erratic actions?"

"I would leave the specifics up to you, but anything that would convince an opponent that you're mentally unstable." I raised my hand to my chin and tapped one finger to it. "You could consider flapping your arms and making bird sounds."

"And you could consider biting me."

I frowned. "Another human expression?"

She didn't answer, instead unfolding her arms and putting them on her hips. "You want me to run around flapping my arms and making noises like a bird while you'll be doing what?"

"Approaching from the other direction and preparing to attack."

"I hate this plan."

Now I crossed my arms over my chest, my hands brushing the woven steel of my sash. "Do you have another suggestion?"

"Something better than me running around in an arena in front of hundreds of aliens pretending to be a deranged bird?" She pursed her lips and twisted them to one side. "Give me some time, and I'm sure I can come up with something that isn't completely humiliating."

Her fierce expression almost made me laugh. Tyrria irritated was almost as much of a turn-on as when she was flushed with exertion. The familiar spark of desire roiled in my gut, but I forced it down and ripped my gaze away.

More than any strategy or plan, our survival depended on me keeping my mating fever dormant. If I failed at that, all was lost for both of us.

CHAPTER
FIFTEEN

Tyrria

I was still steamed when I left Naz, but I hadn't come up with a better plan than me making an absolute idiot of myself to distract the other fighters while Naz attacked them. I despised the idea of running around flapping my arms—and what kind of bird noises would be most distracting, chirping or squawking?—but I had to admit that it would probably work. That is, until word got around that I wasn't deranged or believed that I was a bird.

I held the tray steady as I walked past the guards stationed on either side of the door with their batons at the ready. They glanced at me but didn't do much more than grunt at me when they saw I was clearing the empty carafes. The batons weren't for me. Their easy dismissal was an unpleasant reminder that they didn't need to worry about me escaping, not when I wore an electrified collar around my throat.

SUBDUE

Even without moving my neck, the metal was cool on my skin and a constant presence. When I'd been in the battle ring or grappling with Naz I'd forgotten that it existed but as soon as the distractions vanished, the awareness of the ring returned, along with the hard knot in my gut. No matter what the Taori said, escaping wasn't going to be as simple as he liked to make it out to be. Not if he truly planned to take me with him.

It would be smarter for him to escape alone. He'd have a better chance getting out and staying alive without me. The thought was terrifying, but also comforting because it was true. I'd been taught to embrace the truth, even if it hurt. It had been a skill I'd learned at my father's knee. He'd never been a dreamer. That had been my mother, although I only knew that from stories. My father had embraced the hard reality of life, and he's made sure I understood it every moment of my childhood.

But he promised, a little voice whispered in the back of my head, as I walked down the brightly lit hallway with colorful beams dappling the floor. The dreamer inside me only ever whispered, her voice timid and afraid of being too loud and then silenced forever.

Promises aren't real, I reminded myself. They're only words, and words come and go.

I pressed my lips together, fighting the urge to actually snap back. I knew I shouldn't trust in what the Taori had vowed, but I couldn't help it. His certainty was contagious, and hope fluttered in my belly like a glow fly with its diaphanous wings that seemed too small to keep its illuminated body aloft.

After a few more turns down the corridor, I realized that I'd forgotten the way to the kitchens. I paused and was about to turn back and retrace my steps—this time I would not be distracted by my wandering thoughts—when a voice from behind startled me.

"I was hoping I'd see you today."

I bobbled my tray, leveling it before one of the carafes tipped over, and turned to see the doe-eyed female from my first day smiling at me. She also carried a tray, although hers was filled with empty plates of bones stripped clean.

I released a breath and managed a smile. "Are you heading to the kitchens? I forgot the way."

She nodded and fell in step with me. "You're heading in the right direction. It's around this corner." She scanned me quickly and nodded. "You look like you're doing okay." She lowered her voice as if we weren't the only ones in the corridor. "I heard what happened in the arena. We all did."

I didn't know if her disapproving look was because I'd been put in the battle ring, or because of Naz going primal. "It was unexpected."

She shook her head and her dark curls swung around her face. "We're here to attend the fighters. Not be thrown in as fodder."

I didn't tell her that it wasn't a one-time thing as far as Naz and I were concerned. That would only send the woman into a panic. Who was to say that the Xulonians wouldn't start showing all the female attendants into the arena?

"I guess the beast saved you, though." She nodded approvingly. "I know Carina wasn't sad that the Zarnock was killed. She hated attending him. He's one of those fighters you deliver the food to and then make yourself scarce."

"Carina?" Had I been told any of the names of the other attendants? So much had happened since I arrived it was a bit of a blur.

"You didn't meet her." The brunette met my eyes for a beat. "I'm Kensie, by the way."

"Tyrria."

We rounded the corner, and I breathed in the savory scent of food. The dishes that were prepared for the fighters weren't Kayling dishes, so it wasn't familiar food, but it still made my mouth water. Naz and I had been so busy training me that we'd forgotten to stop for lunch, working straight through the day after a light breakfast. By now, my stomach was rumbling, and I was sure he was starving.

I followed the female through tall, arched doors where the aroma of food clung to the hot air and there was a cacophony of chopping, clattering, and talking. Stoves lined one wall, and they were attended by a green-skinned alien species I didn't recognize. Steam billowed from bubbling pots and smoke curled into the air from meat sizzling on wide grills.

The kitchens had a high, domed ceiling but there were no windows letting in bright light. Instead, there were vents cut into the roof through which the smoke and steam could escape. Even so, the stone walls were coated with grease and the ceiling was darkened from soot.

"She's alive!"

I followed the loud voice that rose above the sounds of cooks shouting and pans clattering. The blonde I'd met my first day waved at me as she stood, filling a tureen with some kind of brown, chunky stew. I grinned back and followed Kensie to where the blonde stood.

"I'm alive," I said, stating the obvious and feeling a bit silly. It was nice that the other female attendants had been worried about me or had even thought about me at all. I'd only come to the kitchens once since I'd been assigned to Naz, and no other attendants had been here then, so I'd assumed I might never see them again.

"We heard what happened," the blonde said with wide eyes.

"She knows," Kensie said, elbowing the woman aside. "Tyrria, this is Bobbie."

"I remember," I said, gaining me a smile from the blonde.

"What I want to know is if the beast is a beast everywhere," Bobbie said, moving her eyebrows up and down with a wicked grin.

Kensie rolled her eyes as she ladled some of the stew into a smaller tureen. "Not all of us do that kind of thing. This isn't the lust moon. It's not like they're watching and giving us bonuses."

"Too bad," Bobbie muttered with a wink to me. "I wouldn't mind a bonus. I'll bet your beast has lots of bonuses."

My cheeks warmed even though I knew the woman was only teasing me. "I...I wouldn't know about any of that."

Bobbie let out a tormented sigh. "Too bad. I heard he went primal in the arena—and that he has horns and a tail." She gave a small shudder. "I'd take that any day over my new fighter."

"What's your new fighter like?" Kensie asked, her brow wrinkling in concern. "He isn't a Zarnock or a Berrian, is he?"

Bobbie made a face. "No, he's a Xerxen."

"A Xerxen?" I'd heard of the species but didn't remember details.

"They're small and spindly," Bobbie said. "But their skin is poisonous to the touch for most other species, so the fights aren't pretty. Lots of burning flesh and screaming." Then she slapped a hand over her mouth. "Oops. I probably shouldn't have said that." She held up a pair of long, white gloves. "I'm off to serve dinner and try not to get burned myself."

"Be careful," Kensie called after the woman as she left with her tray of food. Then she turned back to me. "My fighter probably won't win his fight but at least he isn't poisonous."

It hadn't occurred to me all the different types of aliens at

SUBDUE

the arena. Once again, I was glad I'd been assigned to the Taori, even if I wished neither of us were stuck on the alien moon.

"From what I've heard," Kensie said, handing me an empty tureen, "your fighter could go the distance."

"What does that mean?" I asked, taking the ladle from her and scooping stew into my tureen. "I thought they liked new fighters all the time."

"They do, but the crowd gets favorites. Sometimes a fighter is so good that he can't be defeated by any of the other opponents." She frowned. "Then they let all the other fighters take him on at once in a big, final battle."

A bloodbath was more like it, I thought, as my gut twisted, and I accidentally sloshed some stew onto my tray. It didn't matter how good you were. They would kill you anyway.

I thought about Naz's revenge list. Time to start crossing off names.

CHAPTER
SIXTEEN

Naz

I strode nervously around the room, my tail twitching as I darted glances at the door and willed Tyrria to return, so I would know she was safe. It wasn't that I didn't believe that she would be allowed to walk freely throughout the arena complex. The electrified collar ringing her neck assured the guards she wouldn't escape. Regardless, I didn't trust the twisted aliens not to use the female as a pawn to manipulate even more than they had.

My pulse quickened as I thought about how effectively the aliens had weakened me without even knowing it. I might still be a deadly fighter—even more so when Tyrria was in the ring with me—but I could no longer escape without bringing her with me. I didn't doubt my own cunning or even brute force in overpowering the guards and finding a way off the moon, but I refused to harm Tyrria in the process. That meant that until I discovered how to disarm or remove her collar, there would be no leaving the battle moon.

I growled low, rage pulsing through me. I was furious at the Xulonians and the guards they used to enact their will, but I was also angry with myself. I could have remained focused on my mission and not allowed myself to be distracted by the female. That would have been the prudent course of action, considering that I needed to find my crew. My heart twisted in my chest at the thought of my Taori brothers being in danger, or being tormented on one of the other moons. I refused to suffer the fate of my father, who'd failed at his job of protector to his crew.

"Escape," I growled under my breath. "Focus on escape."

I tipped back my head, scanning the smooth, high walls and the domed ceiling. Even if I could reach the glass dome, the colored surface looked thicker than transparent glass, and I feared it would be nearly impossible to break with even my brute strength. The upper level of the arena complex was bright and light-filled, but the allure of the interior masked the fact that there was no easy way out. I preferred this room to the subterranean dungeon I'd started in, but it was still my prison.

I eyed the door again, remembering that there were two guards with electrified batons flanking the outside. They would be no match for my strength and battle cunning, but the batons made the task of defeating them harder. Then there was the matter of Tyrria. All they had to do was threaten to zap her collar, and any attempt to escape would be over.

"Tyrria." I husked out her name like it was both a curse and a prayer, as thoughts of the female flooded my brain.

My skin sizzled with heat that moved across it like flames

licking a burning log. My fingers tingled, and carnal need coiled in my belly like a snake waiting to strike. My cock thickened even as I tried to calm my body's response to my fury, and to thoughts of the female with pale pink hair.

"I am Taori," I gritted out, as if the words might douse the fever that was as ancient and powerful as any litany I could recite.

Now was not the time to stir the fever. It had been hard enough when I'd been grappling with the female, and it had taken every bit of my self-control not to allow myself to succumb to the fiery embrace of the Quaibyn. It would be so natural to allow the fever to take over my body like it was meant to, like it had so many times before.

My mind drifted back to my first Quaibyn when I'd just come of age. I'd been attended by priestesses on Taor who covered me with fragrant oils that cooled my skin as they took turns with me, chanting Taori incantations and poetry until I'd finally locked one in the mating clench. Even that powerful memory came only in snatches, as I'd always lost myself to the Quaibyn and remembered only hazy moments of the fever.

I groaned as my swollen cock ached even more. Thinking about past fevers was no way to fight off this one, so I closed my eyes and thought of the corpulent bartender at the outpost on Ventria Prime. His gapped teeth had been mossy and his breath foul—the last creature I could ever find arousing.

"Better," I murmured as I hissed out a breath and sensed my cock retreating. As soon as we returned to our time and that galaxy, I'd have to find the Grendellian bartender and thank him.

"I hope you're in the mood for stew, or chunky soup, or whatever this is," Tyrria said, as she bustled into the room. She barely glanced my way as she placed the tray on the central table and began to unload the contents, which appeared to be

SUBDUE

a blue ceramic tureen, a pair of bowls, a loaf of bread on a board and the refilled water and wine carafes. "I'm not sure where the recipe comes from, but it smells good."

She was right. The savory scent of the stew drifted to me, reminding me that grappling with the female and suppressing the fever worked up a significant appetite. I stood and joined her at the table as she filled the bowls and tore off hunks of bread.

I took a bowl from her as she continued talking.

"Good news. I saw some of the other female attendants in the kitchens and learned a bit about their fighters. The Xerxen look wimpy, but their skin is poisonous, so don't grab them." She took a bite of bread before carrying her bowl to the table. "I know that's not very helpful, especially since they make you fight in that ridiculous pair of shorts that covers nothing, but at least you know." She took a quick breath. "Kensie says her fighter is easy to beat and not poisonous, so fingers crossed we get him first."

I sat down and started eating, enjoying the patter of her voice as she gave me the details on all the other fighters. Some of the tidbits were useful but most of the fighters sounded like they were severely outmatched and should have never ended up in a battle arena. I pushed aside the ache in my chest for the innocents I would have to kill if I wanted to survive.

When Tyrria took a mouthful of stew, I swallowed my bite of warm, yeasty bread and looked up at her. "Does this mean you've come up with a better battle strategy for us to use in the arena?"

"Better than the crazy bird-lady plan?" She tilted her head at me and grinned then shook her head. "Nope. I think that might just work, but I have an idea that might make it even more distracting."

Before I could ask her for details, the door swung open, and a pair of guards lumbered inside the room. They eyed us sitting together at the table and scowled. "You'll have to finish your food later. It's time to fight." Then one of them barked out a hard laugh. "Both of you."

CHAPTER SEVENTEEN

Tyrria

"I'm having second thoughts about the deranged bird plan," I whispered as we walked side by side down the corridor with two guards in front of us and two bringing up the rear.

"Is that what we're calling it?"

One of the thick-necked guards in front swiveled his head around and frowned at us, grunting as he turned back. They weren't thrilled with us since we'd had to change into the battle garb they insisted on, and I'd complained vehemently about the ridiculous, skimpy costume they'd deemed appropriate for a female to wear to fight.

"A good argument could be made that I now look like a bird," I grumbled as I cut my gaze to the black, gauzy fabric that barely covered all my important bits and fluttered around my legs as I walked. The top was form-fitting and cropped above my naval, leaving my arms and midriff bare and me hoping that the fighter we'd be meeting did not have poisonous skin. The skirt hung low on my hips and had high slits up both thighs, which did make it easier to move. Even so, it could have never been considered good battle attire.

Naz allowed his gaze to linger on me for a moment. "I have seen no bird as pretty as you, but the outfit will help with our distraction."

As I noticed the pupils ringing his ice-blue eyes flare, I wondered if he was referring to distracting our opponent or him.

"We didn't practice your plan," I reminded him. We'd gone over many defensive moves and ways for me to fend of attacks, but the strategy of distraction wasn't something we'd rehearsed. "How do I know when I should become a distraction?"

The Taori gave a choked laugh. "I do not think you will be able to control how much of a distraction you will be, but I will give you a signal when you should distract our opponent on purpose."

Before I could ask him what the signal would be, we'd reached the arched entrance to the arena. My pulse fluttered, and I rubbed my sweaty palms on my sheer skirt, wishing there was more fabric.

I hated that I was going into the battle ring looking every bit the Lycithian pleasurer. I suspected that was the point of my revealing outfit. Make the Xulonians think that I was a full-blooded, shape-shifting Lycithian, known for being prized as the galaxy's most skilled pleasurers. I clenched my teeth together, wishing for the hundredth time in my life that I was a true Lycithian who could shift my form at will. If I was, I would have made sure the Kayling children were too scared of me to bully me like they had. If I was a full-blood Lycithian, I would have already changed into the most violent beast imaginable and torn the guards to bits before turning my wrath on the Xulonian crowd.

I curled my hands into fists. Dreaming about what I wished was pointless. I wasn't the creature I wished I was, and there was no changing that now.

Naz reached for my hand and gave my tight fist a quick squeeze before we were pushed from the relative calm, dimness of the corridor into the blistering light and raucous sounds of the arena. It took my eyes a few beats to adjust to the sun streaming through the glass dome and radiating heat off the dirt floor.

I coughed from the dust we'd kicked up when we'd been pushed from the archway, swiping the back of my hand across my eyes and peering into the packed stands that quivered and buzzed like an angry nest of Cynthian wasps. Wide-mouthed, red faces screamed at us, with spindly arms flailing in the air as if they were the ones being tortured.

It was hard to hear over the roar of the crowd, but Naz yanked me closer to him as he positioned himself in front of me and pivoted both of us in a circle so we could take in the entire battle ring. At first, I saw nothing, and I released a relieved breath. Then I spotted a male being pushed into the ring from the opposite entrance.

Naz stiffened beside me as he also saw the fighter enter, and he bent his knees in a battle stance and tucked me firmly behind him. My gaze went to the viewing box near the other fighter's entrance, and I squinted to see which female attendant occupied it.

"Don't be Bobbie," I whispered to myself. As much faith as

I had in the Taori's skills and experience, poisoned skin was something I'd rather avoid.

Luckily, Bobbie's wavy, blonde hair was distinctive, and the female in the box had dark red hair that hung in straight sheets around her shoulders. We were not fighting the Xerxen. I was also relieved that we weren't facing off against Kensie's fighter, but only because she seemed content with attending him.

I wasn't delusional enough to think that the other females in the arena were my friends, but they'd been kind to me, and I couldn't help wanting their lives to be easier. None of us had deserved to be abducted by aliens and dumped on the battle moon to be servants.

The female in the box wasn't one I recognized, but then again, I hadn't been there long, and I'd only visited the kitchens twice. I'd come to realize that there were quarters for the fighters ringing the huge arena, and fights going on almost all the time, which meant that there were many more fighters and attendants than I'd first thought. According to Kensie, not all the fights garnered big crowds, but the smaller ones eliminated the weaker fighters so that the top contenders worked their way up quickly. Bile churned in my gut as I imagined how much profit the Xulonians were making on the labor and death of innocent creatures.

I swung my gaze back to the fighter who was advancing on us. He was almost as tall as Naz, but not as muscular. While dark ink covered most of the Taori's smooth body, this creature was covered in short, dark hair. The hair on his head was thick and matted, and a beard covered his face. It couldn't hide the menacing grin or the way he licked his lips as he looked at me.

"Lycithian."

I couldn't hear the word emerge from his lips over the screams of the spectators, but I could read his lips. My stomach tightened and prickles danced over my skin. The Taori might not know the reputation of Lycithian females, but this fighter did.

I didn't think I would need to work very hard to distract him. Not with the way he was eyeing me like he wished to devour me. Even over the noise of the crowds that was reverberating through my bones, I felt more than heard Naz growl beside me.

The fighter facing us stood on two legs, but his hands and feet were larger than those of a human, and his ears were large and pointed. I wondered if he was also a hybrid of two species.

While I was contemplating if he could be a descendant of the he-wolf kings of Vondillia, Naz rushed forward in attack. I was startled, but the other fighter wasn't. He crouched with lightning speed, leapt high into the air, and landed behind Naz.

I backed away quickly, thinking that I might be right about the Vondillia blood. The other fighter moved like he was part wolf, and when he bared his sharp fangs at me, fear iced my flesh.

"Lycithian," he rasped again, but this time I heard the deep timbre of his voice and the hunger in it.

He advanced on me, but didn't get far before Naz was on him, circling his neck with his arm and yanking him back. The fighter snarled as he struggled, finally loosening the Taori's arm enough for him to sink his sharp, pointed teeth into.

Naz roared, flipping the fighter over him to loosen the bite, and sending him sprawling to the ground. Blood spilled freely from the kalesh's forearm, and he slapped his hand over the cut to staunch the flow.

I ran to his side, my heart in my throat at the sight of so much blood. I ripped off a strip of fabric from my skirt and tied it quickly around his arm to slow the bleeding.

"I am fine," he grunted, although his voice was strained. "You should not stay near me."

I whirled around as the fighter advanced on us, a dark rumble vibrating my own chest as I swiped at him with long, bladed claws where my hands used to be. "Screw that."

CHAPTER EIGHTEEN

Naz

My arm throbbed with pain as I held my hand over the gash. Blood seeped through my fingers, even though Tyrria's makeshift tourniquet had slowed the flow to a trickle.

She stood in front of me as the fighter raced toward us, as if she could prevent another attack. I'd seen the way the creature eyed her, but I doubted even his naked desire would not keep him from tearing into me again—if I let him live long enough for that. Already my blood was simmering, the rage ignited by my innate urge to protect the female. He might have wounded me, but now I knew his tactical advantages. I would not fall victim to his fangs again.

"I am fine," I told Tyrria, pushing aside the pain and tightening my jaw. "You should not stay near me."

She ignored me, spinning to face him. "Screw that."

I reached up to block the attack, but my arm froze as Tyrria lifted her own arm to swipe at the fighter, long metallic blades flashing from clawed hands. I almost glanced behind us, but there was no other fighter in the ring. The claws and the blades that sliced across the alien's chest were hers.

The creature cried out in pain and fell to the ground as I curled my body over Tyrria's and wrapped her now deadly hands beneath us. Had the crowd seen what she'd done—what she'd become? It had happened so fast, and we'd been so close together that I could only hope they'd assumed that the strike had come from me.

Tyrria's body trembled as I held her, her gaze locked on her hands, which had returned to normal. I had to blink a few times to reassure myself there weren't pointed blades protruding from between her knuckles or that I hadn't gone mad for a moment.

I glanced at the fighter on the ground. Blood was pouring from deep gashes in his belly that did not come from me, so I knew I hadn't imagined it. Tyrria had sprouted blades from her hands, and they'd vanished as quickly as they'd appeared.

She peered up at me, confusion and panic etched in her face. She was as shocked as I was, but neither of us had time to dwell on that. The crowd had gasped when the fighter had dropped from his leap through the air and now they were cheering and booing as he attempted to stand while holding one hand to his bloody belly.

The carnal hunger in his eyes had been replaced by fear and pain, but he was still standing and advancing. He might be wounded, but the creature wasn't down for the count. We were both dripping blood and in pain, and the sharp, coppery scent of our blood made my nose twitch.

"You have distracted him enough, Tyrria." I pulled her to

her feet and tucked her behind me. "Now you need to let me finish him."

She nodded, clearly still shaken from her transformation. I'd have questions for her later, but for now, I needed to focus on the battle.

The other fighter was trailing blood as he walked forward, his agile stride broken and his gait uneven. With each step, he winced, and the pain etched deeper into his face. He was a worthy opponent, and I despised the fact that I had to take his life to save mine.

I stole a glance at the frothing crowd. The aliens I should be killing were the ones in the stands and the ones who escorted us to the arena and stood outside our doors. For a flicker of a moment, I imagined joining forces with this valiant warrior and leaping into the stand in tandem. We would attack the red-skinned creatures without mercy, tearing at their wrath-filled faces and ripping off the arms they used to spur on the violence in the battle ring.

That fantasy died a quick death when I remembered the steel collar ringing Tyrria's neck. I doubted I would reach the first Xulonian spectator before she would be shocked—or maybe killed—by the guards. I swallowed down the bitter taste of temperance as I reminded myself that I would have to bide my time.

I'd allowed myself to scan the arena when we'd entered. There was no obvious means of escape from the massive battle ring. The stands extended high, and then the dome stretched over that. Aside from the entrances for the fighters, I'd spotted no other ways to enter the arena. I hadn't determined how the spectators entered, but I suspected their entrance would not be easy for a fighter to access. We would not be escaping through the arena, even if I did enjoy the fantasy of taking down as many of the enemy as possible as I left.

Swinging my head back to my opponent, I took a deep breath and steeled myself for my task. The battles were to the death. There was no other way to survive and fight another day. It was him or me—and Tyrria. Thinking of the female made it easier to push aside my remorse. I was fighting for her and my crew, as much as for myself. I'd made a vow to both of them that I refused to break.

"I share in the tears and sorrow for your falling," I murmured, locking eyes with the fighter.

As if he'd heard my words and understood them, his step faltered. Then he hardened his mouth into a line that vanished beneath his thick beard and clutched his hand tighter into his stomach, rushing forward as if he wasn't wounded.

His fast movement caught me off guard and I dove to one side, snatching Tyrria's arm and pulling her with me—but not fast enough. The other fighter tackled her to the ground and the two of them rolled across the ground until they came to a stop, and he jerked her to her feet in front of him. His blood had smeared across her bare arms and belly, and dust coated the gauzy fabric of her clothing.

Seeing his blood marking her skin and his open mouth pressed to her neck, his fangs nicking her skin and drawing droplets of blood, made the fire stoking hot in my core blaze to life. The heat scorched through my body like a tidal wave of rage, and my skin sizzled as if a forge had been fired within me.

He ran his hairy hands up the outside of her thigh, bunching the fabric as he went. The crowd was like a writhing beast chanting for blood, but all I could see gyrating behind him and Tyrria was red. Blood pounded in my ears as the red haze consumed me, and everything turned to red—the crowd, the arena, my opponent dripping blood as he touched the female. My female.

She stood completely still with her gaze pinned to me, but

there was a warning in her eyes. She shook her head imperceptibly, but it still earned her a deeper nick from the creature's fangs. As I watched that drop of blood ooze from her neck and wind down the pale skin of her throat, my eyes rolled back in my head.

The red haze gave way to black, and the chanting of the crowd became a blaring shriek in my own head as I slashed and tore, moving without conscious thought but with one pulsing urge. To reclaim what was mine.

CHAPTER NINETEEN

Tyrria

What had just happened? Blood marred my skin, and my clothes were once again torn to bits and barely clinging to my body as Naz carried me over his shoulder from the arena. This time, I was barely aware of the scorching heat emanating from the Taori's skin or the rough, animalistic sounds rumbling from his throat.

Now that I knew about his mating fever and how it was triggered, his second descent into a blood-soaked rage wasn't as shocking. That wasn't to say I hadn't been stunned when he'd lunged for the fighter with such speed and brute force that the creature's head snapped back so hard from the impact of his punch that its neck broke instantly.

Even though he'd flopped to the ground limp and lifeless, Naz hadn't stopped his assault. I don't think he'd realized the fighter was dead as he leapt on the inert body and began pummeling it. Blood had spurted from the open wound on the creature's gut until even that had slowed.

The Xulonian spectators had cheered with every punch and splatter of bright red blood onto the packed dirt floor, but after a while I hadn't known which blood was the other fighter's and which was from Naz. Like before, his horns were speckled with scarlet dots of blood, and it was smeared on his chest.

His roars had been unintelligible as he'd attacked the alien, and even when I'd pulled at his arm to get him to stop, he'd been too deep in the fever to hear me. When he'd stopped, his chest heaving, he'd swiveled around to me, growled in apparent satisfaction, and thrown me over his shoulder.

Now, guards stared with dangling jaws as we passed, and female attendants gaped openly while flattening themselves against the pristine walls. If I didn't have other things racing through my mind, I might have had the same worries they did. Was he out of control? Had the fever made him deadly to even me? But more urgent questions tugged at my brain.

What had happened with my hands? I held them up and examined them as I hung down Naz's back. They looked just as they always had—five fingers on each one, pale skin, unvarnished nails. But for a few moments during the fight, they'd transformed into claws with sharp blades protruding from between the knuckles. Hadn't they?

Although there were no markings on my skin to indicate that anything like that had happened, the other fighter had suffered significant lacerations across his stomach. Cuts that the Taori, despite his ferocity, couldn't have inflicted. Besides, he hadn't even been affected by the fever at that point.

It wasn't impossible, of course. I was half Lycithian. But I'd always been told that being a half-blood meant I couldn't shape shift like my mother and the rest of her species. Any powers I might have inherited had been diluted by my father's Kayling blood. "And the only powers any of them have is the power to judge."

Sure, I'd experienced small shifts growing up. It happened when I was upset or threatened—like you were in the battle ring, I reminded myself—but it hadn't happened enough for me to believe it was something I could control. Luckily, it also hadn't happened enough for any of the Kayling, especially my father, to notice. If they'd thought I could shift, they would have labeled me an even bigger freak than they already had, and I'd have probably been shipped away sooner.

The Taori's feet smacked against the shiny floor as he stalked down the corridor to our quarters, but I was barely paying attention anymore. Not even when the two guards flanking the doors shrank at our arrival and backed away.

The only creatures who'd witnessed me shifting before were a rabid Gurly-cat, who'd probably been as shocked as me when the skin on my arms had become hard and scaly and impossible for its bites to penetrate, and the sea creatures who'd witnessed me grow gills and a tail when I'd gotten my foot stuck in seaweed and been pulled underwater in the Kayling sea. My heart raced as I thought about how both times, shifting had saved my life without me even trying to do it or thinking about shifting into a different creature. Now my ability had saved me again.

My chest swelled as the reality hit me. If I could shift without thinking about it, what was to say I couldn't do it at will? I'd learned enough by now that my father couldn't be trusted. I'd taken his word that I had no powers, but that had been a lie. I did have powers. Powers he'd probably been afraid of and wanted to suppress in me.

Anger flared hot inside me, but then I brushed it aside. I didn't want to spend another moment thinking about how I'd been betrayed by my father and any other male I'd ever trusted. That was in the past. They weren't a part of my life, and never would be again. I wanted to focus on my newfound power. I was a Lycithian who could shape-shift. This changed everything.

"I'm a fucking shaper-shifter," I said as Naz swung me down onto the bed.

He hitched in ragged breath as he looked at me, finally speaking for the first time since he'd snapped in the battle ring. "Mine."

Then he scraped his hands through his hair, the silver glinting through the black, and staggered back, as if some part of the Taori kalesh inside was preventing him from acting on the fever that was clearly ravaging his body.

My own flesh burned from my newfound sense of power, and the burst of desire I felt for the only male I'd ever known who'd defended me with his own life more than once and was, even now, shielding me from the danger of himself.

"Don't go," I said, my voice trembling. "I don't want you to stop yourself."

He slowly lifted his gaze to meet mine, and the raw need in his eyes made my mouth go dry.

"I *am* yours," I told him, knowing that in that moment, at least, it was true.

CHAPTER
TWENTY

Naz

The rushing torrent of blood in my ears muffled her words, but I dropped my gaze and followed the movements of her pink lips. Had she told me not to go? My pulse jack-knifed and my heart hammered so quickly it felt like it might burst from my ribcage.

"I am yours."

Those words I heard, even if they were soft and pleading. I shook my head as if shaking them off. Tyrria didn't know what she was saying. She was sacrificing herself to help me, and I didn't want pity. Not from her. If I couldn't have her heart, I didn't want to torment myself with anything else she could give me. My fever might be quenched, but I would know the difference.

"No." I forced the words out through clenched teeth. "I don't accept."

SUBDUE

Her eyebrows popped up. "You don't want me?"

I curled my hands into fists so tight that my short fingernails bit into my flesh. "Not like this. I refuse to allow you to sacrifice your virtue to my fever."

I jerked my body away from her, so she couldn't see that my cock was thickening at the thought of being with her and straining against the snug fabric of the battle shorts. My skin was so hot that the bits of it not covered by dark, swirling ink were red. My head swam even as the haze of rage that had blanketed my eyes faded. I no longer craved blood to slake my fury, but the sticky streaks on my flesh told me I'd exacted my due.

As much as I desired Tyrria, I needed to rid myself of the blood staining my body and reminding me that the Quaibyn was advancing without mercy. Soon I would be unable to resist her, even if I wished to preserve her honor, and I would not return from the violent haze.

Staggering away from her, I plunged into the sunken pool. The heat stung as I submerged my cuts and gashes, but the water washed the blood and dirt from my skin. It might be hot, but it still subdued my urgent desire and cleared the final bits of haze from my brain.

"Who said I was sacrificing anything?"

I turned at Tyrria's sharp question to see her standing at the edge of the pool with her hands on her waist and one hip jutted to the side.

"You wish to help me cure the fever, don't you?"

She shrugged one shoulder. "Did it ever occur to you that I might just want to know what it's like to ride a cock as big as yours?"

My jaw dropped. It hadn't occurred to me. Although some pleasurers had shown appreciation for our three-crowned cocks, there had been more than a few females who'd been genuinely shocked and terrified by the sight. The halflings of the planet Jalen had almost fainted en masse.

Tyrria started pulling off the remaining torn bits of her outfit, shedding the scraps of the top and then tugging the black wisps of sheer cloth down her hips. She let them fall to the floor and puddle around her feet.

I should have averted my eyes, but I couldn't. She was too beautiful, and I couldn't resist devouring the sight of her creamy skin and the pale pink wisps of hair between her legs. Even the nipples of her tear-drop shaped breasts were pink, something I'd never seen on an alien female before.

The bloodthirsty urge to protect her might have receded into the dark recesses of my brain, but the hungry desire to possess her stormed through me just as hard and fast. Despite the spicy scent of the bubbling water, the Quaibyn gave me the heightened senses to smell the sweetness of her arousal and hear the thudding of her heart. Maybe she wasn't making the sacrifice I thought she was.

"You do not have to..." I started to say, even as I moved to the edge of the pool to be nearer to her, the intoxicating sight and scent of her drawing me like a magnet.

Tyrria dropped down so that her legs were dangling in the water as her ass balanced on the edge. "I'm not doing this for you, Taori." Her silver eyes almost glowed. "I'm doing this for me."

"You wish to...?"

She parted her knees and used her feet to hook around my waist and tug me forward. "We just defeated another opponent in the battle ring, and I discovered that I'm a lot more than I was told I was, so I think we both deserve a reward." Her gaze drifted beneath the water. "A big one."

My heart had resumed its insistent drumbeat, and my skin tingled as if it was burning. I bit my bottom lip until I tasted the tang of blood. "I cannot control the fever if you continue to talk like that."

She gave me a wicked smile and ran a finger down my damp chest, the tip bumping across the ridges of my stomach. She leaned close to me, and her lips feathered warm breath across my ear. "Who said I wanted you to control anything, kalesh?"

Hearing her whisper my Taori title snapped something inside me. I palmed the back of her head in my hand and tangled my fingers through her hair, as I crashed my mouth onto hers in a claiming kiss. My lips moved firmly against hers as she yielded to me, releasing a breathy moan as I parted her lips with my tongue and delved deeper into her mouth. She tasted as sweet as she smelled, and my head swam with need as I savored her mouth and her tongue and the pattering of her heart.

I finally tore my mouth from hers. "I have to taste more of you."

Tyrria's lips were swollen from my kisses and her eyes half-lidded as she ran both hands through my hair and pushed my head down. With a hungry growl, I obliged her, tracing my tongue down the soft skin of her throat until I reached her breasts. I sucked each pebbled, pink nipple as she arched her back and thrust them deeper into my mouth. Then I reluctantly released them and continued kissing my way down her body until I sank to my knees in the water and parted her legs.

"I've never come on anyone's tongue before," she said as she curled her fingers tighter in my hair.

"An irresistible challenge," I murmured.

My cock ached, but I needed to taste her as much as I needed to fuck her. The fever hungered for her juices, the beast inside me needing to scent her before I filled her. I tugged down my shorts under the water, though, and let my cock spring free. I dragged one hand down the length of it, my fingers stroking each crown briefly before I grabbed Tyrria by the ass and yanked her closer to my mouth.

With a startled yelp, her legs fell open. I groaned with pleasure at the sight of her pink petals before I buried my face in them. My knees almost buckled as I licked at her slippery honey, her sounds of pleasure fueling the carnal fire that was smoldering inside me and threatening to burn me alive. When I found her small bundle of nerves and started to swirl my tongue over it, her body writhed beneath me, and her hips twitched.

"Your tongue feels so good," she gasped. "But I want you inside me."

I gripped her ass cheeks and held her to me as I continue to work her with my tongue. The need to impale her on my cock was almost making me lightheaded, but first I needed to feel her come on my tongue. I shook my head between her legs and growled.

Tyrria slid her hands from my hair to my horns and wrapped her legs around my shoulders. My body jerked as her fingers caressed the stripes on my horns and sent ripples of pleasure through me. I shifted one hand from her ass and slipped a finger inside her as I sucked her swollen nub.

"Fuck me," she cried, as her legs trembled.

Soon. Desire pounded out almost every other rational thought but the need to fill her and fuck her until she screamed, and my body locked her in the mating clench. Then she would truly be mine.

CHAPTER
TWENTY-ONE

Tyrria

I arched my back as waves of euphoria cascaded over me. The Taori may never have met a Kayling or a Lycithian, but it was clear he knew how to pleasure females.

I stroked his horns, relishing in the rough, desperate noises he made that vibrated his lips and sent even more jolts through me. I was so close, but the sight of his dark head between my legs as I held onto his striped horns made me want to ride his tongue forever.

I'd never been with a male strictly because I wanted to before. I'd always been trying to prove something—that I was desirable even though I wasn't a full Kayling, that I wasn't something my father could control until he sold me off to the highest bidder, that I wasn't going to go to the imperial officer who bought me as a pristine virgin. Sure, I'd let some of the Kayling boys have their way with me, but I'd been using them, too. They'd satisfied their curiosity to fuck the half-blood, while I'd defied my father and sullied myself before I could be auctioned off.

I'd reveled in how eagerly they'd fucked me, and how amazed they'd been that I wasn't some oddity once my clothes were off. They might have pretended not to know me if they saw me on the street, but when I spread my legs for them, they were in my thrall. It had been a rush to see how I could control them—and an even bigger rush when I rebuffed their advances for the second session they always craved—but it had never been about my pleasure.

I forced away memories of the past, focusing only on the Taori who wanted nothing more than to make me come even as he was being ravaged by a primal fever. Heat radiated off him, and his movements were becoming more urgent as he squeezed my ass and fucked me with his finger. When he growled again, my body detonated.

Tipping my head to the domed, glass ceiling, I closed my eyes as my legs jerked and clamped around his head. I clutched his horns, holding his head to me as I quivered and moaned, finally letting go and flopping back onto the floor.

I only had a moment to savor the aftershocks before Naz was pulling me by the legs into the pool. I let out a small shriek as I was submerged under the hot water but then he was pulling me to him, wrapping my legs around his waist and pressing my chest flush to his. My chest was heaving as I tried to remember how to breathe normally, but the Taori's breath was also jagged.

He touched his forehead to mine, and I saw that his crystal-blue eyes were almost black, as if they had been swallowed by the molten black pupils. He threaded his fingers through my hair and yanked my head back so that my throat was exposed.

He ran a tongue up the length of it and nipped my jawline. "You're going to take my cock now."

It wasn't a question, it was a warning, and an unwanted thrill tickled my spine. Naz's voice was desperate, and his hands trembled as he held me.

I nodded, even as fear made my heart stutter in my chest. "I want it."

"Tell me," he ordered, and I could easily understand how his forceful tone commanded his warriors. "Tell me what you want."

I hesitated, and he nipped me again, this time hard enough to make me flinch.

"I want you to fuck me."

He moaned and twisted his head to one side as his eyes rolled back in his head. "You think you can take being fucked by a Taori?"

"I can take whatever you can give me, Kalesh."

With a ferocious roar, Naz lifted me and notched his cock at my entrance. My feet scrabbled to find purchase on his ass as he used his grip on my hair to tip my head forward so that our eyes were locked as he entered me. His other hand held my hip and moved me down so that I took his long, thick cock in one smooth thrust. The water splashed around our shoulders and sloshed over the sides of the pool.

I opened my mouth to cry out as I took first one, then two, and finally all three cockheads, but the shock had driven all the air from my lungs. My hands slipped on his wet shoulders as I held him for balance and tried to adjust to the intrusion.

I'd bragged I could take him, as if he wasn't significantly larger than any male I'd been with, and I dug my nails into the firm muscles of his shoulders as I absorbed the pain and the pleasure. I'd wanted this. I'd wanted him, and not just because I was curious what such a big, unusual cock would feel like. I'd wanted to experience what it was like to fuck someone I liked, and who aroused my desire.

All my other conquests had been hate fucks. I'd only done them to secretly punish my father—and maybe myself. There had been no affection, or even much attraction. I'd enjoyed seeing the power I had over the Kayling boys, but I'd never desired them, or thought twice about them once I was done. They'd used me, and I'd used them.

Naz was different. He'd asked nothing from me before saving my life and promising to help me escape. He'd even fought whatever animalistic urge was making him burn with fever, resisting the need to claim me even if it would cure him. Not only did I feel my own powerful pull to the Taori, I trusted him. It might go against everything I'd convinced myself about males, but I was sure he was different.

"So tight," Naz ground out as he held himself inside me, his breath escaping his lips in agonized pants.

"It's okay," I whispered. "You can move. I want you to."

"What do you want?" He teased in a voice so velvety it hummed across my skin and made my nipples pucker.

"I want you to show me how a kalesh of the Taori fucks."

Naz's eyes flared as he lifted me and drove me down hard. I cried out but hadn't caught my breath before he was lifting me up again. He dropped his hand from my hair, clutching my hips with both hands and thrusting me up and down on his cock under the water. His pace was frenzied, his expression wild, and his gaze dark and unfocused.

With a move so fast that I barely registered it before I was facing the other direction, he lifted me and spun me around. I threw my arms forward to grip the edge of the pool as he tipped my ass up and entered me from behind. The new angle was even deeper, and Naz grabbed a handful of my short hair, which meant almost all of it, and used it to pull my head back and hold me in place as he thrust into me. When something thick and furry tickled my clit, it took me a few seconds to realize that he was using his tail to rub between my legs as he fucked me.

I twisted my head around to look at him, startled by the long hair falling in his face and the sweat rolling down his corded neck. When he caught me looking at him, his eyes flashed a possessive heat, and he curled his body on top of mine. He inhaled deeply at the base of my neck then licked the shell of my ear as he let out a dark hum. "Mine."

Instead of being offended that he was treating me like his to own, I flushed at the rumble in his chest as he declared I was his. He ran a hand up my stomach until he cupped one breast and rolled the hard nipple between his thumb and finger, as he continued thrusting his cock and working his tail on my clit.

When my second release slammed into me, hot and punishing, I dropped my head between my shoulder blades as I spasmed around the Taori's cock and his tail, quivering and gripping the side of the pool hard. Naz paused for a beat as my pussy clenched him again and again then he used one hand on the small of my back to lower my head and lift my ass. With a bellow that rattled the glass overhead, he stroked into me one last time, holding himself as he pulsed hot inside me.

I drew shaky breaths as I waited for him to pull out, but his cock didn't soften. Instead, it seemed to swell and grow harder. Before I could jerk away, Naz had spun me once again without breaking contact. This time when I faced him, I tried to wiggle from his grasp, but it felt like his cock was stuck inside me. "What—?"

"Don't," he said, wrapping his strong arms around my back. "You can't escape the mating clench."

I stilled, my gaze falling on his, which was no longer wild and unfocused. "The what?"

CHAPTER
TWENTY-TWO

Naz

My heart was resuming its normal pace, but the sweat continued to trickle down my body. I lowered Tyrria into the water with me. Now that my body wasn't boiling, the warm water was soothing.

"The mating clench is part of curing the fever." I brushed a damp strand of her sideswept bangs off her face and let my finger trace a wet line down her temples. "It will pass."

She twitched her hips as if trying to break the lock but flinched when the engorged crown at the base of my cock held her in place. "When? How long are we stuck like this?"

I coiled an arm around her back and one around her ass, lifting her with me as I stepped from the pool. Water streamed from both our bodies as I padded across the floor and lowered us onto the bed. I didn't care that our wet bodies would soak the bedding as I rolled Tyrria onto her back and held myself over her on my elbows. "There isn't a set amount of time."

Her breath hitched in her chest as she shifted her legs up to loop around my waist, making the clench more comfortable. "Are we talking minutes, or astro-days?"

"Not astro-days." I thought back to tales I'd heard of especially long clenches. Not even those had lasted days.

Tyrria eyed me. "That's reassuring."

I studied her flushed cheeks and her heavy breathing. "Are you in pain?"

"No," she answered quickly. "But I've never been stuck like this. Every male I've known is all too eager to roll off and go home."

I wrinkled my brow. "It sounds like you haven't been with worthy males."

"That's an understatement."

Although the fever was no longer licking flames along my skin or sending rage storming through me, my spine tingled with irritation. "You were treated badly by males? If you tell me who they are, I will add their names to my list of vengeance."

This made her laugh, and her body relaxed beneath mine. "You can't kill everyone who's hurt me."

"Why not?" As her mate, it would be my duty to punish anyone who'd wronged her. Being the female who doused my mating fever and was locked to me in the clench didn't make her my mate, but I knew without a doubt that she was meant to be mine. I'd sensed it before, but now I knew it in my bones that our meeting was written in the stars long ago.

"For one, if you don't get your list under control, you'll never get through it. It's more important to take care of the Xulonians and the aliens who are running this place, than to go after a bunch of worthless Kaylings."

I frowned, remembering what she'd told me of herself. "You are Kayling, are you not?"

"Half, but I'd rather focus on my other half."

"Lycip—?"

"Lycithian," she corrected before I finished my attempt at the species name. "My mother was Lycithian, but she died when I was young." Her expression darkened. "My father was Kayling, and he raised me."

"He did not protect you, if it was Kayling males who treated you badly."

Hurt contorted her face for a beat. "No, he didn't. He's the reason I was on the imperial transport that was boarded by the Hettite slavers who sold me to this place."

"I don't understand."

"He'd made a deal for me to be the concubine for some imperial commander. I may only be half Lycithian, but it was enough to tempt the commander and earn my father some credits." Her gaze dropped. "Lycithians are prized as pleasurers."

Shock made me speechless but then fury roiled in my gut. "Your father sold you?"

Tyrria put a hand on my chest. "You still can't kill him."

She was very wrong about that. I could easily kill the dishonorable male and feel not a gram of remorse. "His lack of honor is not your shame to carry. You did nothing wrong."

As soon as I uttered those words, I was reminded of my own father's shame that clung to me. The defeat of his ship had not been my fault, but the legacy was still mine to repair. Maybe Tyrria and I were not carrying such different burdens.

"I was born," she said. "I hope now he's happy to finally be rid of the shame of a half-blood daughter."

I rolled onto one side and pulled her to face me. "You are

beautiful and perfect. Any male—including your father—who doesn't see that is a fool."

She gave me a half grin. "You sure you're not just saying that because you're still inside me?"

I curled an arm around her back and tugged her closer to me. "I say that because it's true. You are the most captivating female I've ever met. But not because of your bloodline." I pressed one palm to the soft skin between her breasts. "Because of you."

Her silver eyes shone as she blinked rapidly. "Thanks. I think you're pretty great, and not only because you made me come two times."

I couldn't fight the smug smile creeping across my face. The feverish heat was receding from my body and a sense of contentment washed over me. It was nothing like I'd ever experienced during the Quaibyn, even with the most experienced priestesses. My cock was still lodged deep inside her, but it throbbed with the urge to move, which was impossible until the clench released.

"That was only the beginning." I rolled her onto her back again, so I was on top of her, and I feathered a kiss across her lips. "I plan to hear your cries of pleasure much more in the future."

A sigh slipped from her mouth as she wrapped her arms around my neck and brushed her fingers along the back curls of my horns, sending shockwaves down my spine. "That goes double for you."

CHAPTER
TWENTY-THREE

Tyrria

I was glad to be back in normal clothing. Normal by alien battle moon standards, at least. The soft, blue cloth draped loosely across my collarbone and was ruched at the waist before spilling to my ankles. I hadn't found any pants in the wardrobe, but I was glad I didn't have Naz's scant choices—or have to wear barely-there battle shorts in the arena.

My thoughts naturally drifted to the Taori I'd left in bed, as I walked down the corridor with an empty tray to fetch breakfast. I didn't know when the mating clench had released us, but by then we were already rolling around in bed, our lips locked and our hands wandering. My face warmed at the memory of finally flopping back on the damp sheets and panting for breath as Naz had done the same. Then he'd curled his body around the back of mine and wrapped his arms around me so that I could rest my head on one bicep like it was a pillow. I'd drifted to sleep cocooned by his warmth and the steady thud of his heartbeat echoing through my own body. The mating clench had been unnerving, but I'd never felt so safe falling asleep in the kalesh's arms.

"Some males *can* be trusted, I guess." The words were said in such a hush no one could have heard them, but I still cast a guilty glance around the empty hallway. It seemed crazy to put my faith in someone I'd only just met, but it also felt completely right. I might not have known the Taori for years, but I already knew he was a better creature than any of the males on Kayling. I also knew without a flicker of doubt that he would protect me and get me off the moon with him.

What happened next sent flutters dancing in my belly. In all the dreams I'd had of leaving Kayling and starting my own life free of the judgment and shame of the planet, I'd never imagined that life being with a partner. Definitely not a male. I'd always envisioned being a solo adventurer, but now the idea of having a partner wasn't so scary. It even felt comforting in an odd way.

I wouldn't mind waking up to Naz every day, I thought, the heat of my cheeks flaming as I remembered our moans and bodies mingling. Or spending a lot more time in bed with him —or in the bath or on the floor.

Then my thoughts slid from Naz to the reason I'd succumbed to his dominant desires. The rush of power I'd experienced knowing that I could shift still made me feel invincible, despite my current situation. I hadn't tested out my powers again, but I felt different—and it wasn't just from being fucked until I was sore.

I glanced at the knuckles curling around the edges of the tray and slowed to a stop. No one was around to see, so I concentrated as hard as I could on my hands, almost dropping the tray when sharp points began to emerge between my joints. I'd startled myself so much that the shift stopped, and my hands returned to normal, but my heart raced with the possibilities. I wasn't a powerless half-blood. I was a Lycithian shapeshifter.

"Up yours, dad," I muttered to myself, reveling in the fact that my father would have hated knowing I was more Lycithian than Kayling. It was everything he'd most feared, which made me happier than I'd been in a long time.

"It is you!" Kensie giggled as she approached from behind with fast, pattering steps. "I knew it had to be. No one else has your gorgeous pink hair. Didn't you hear me call you?"

I gave her an apologetic smile, my cheeks now flaming in embarrassment. "Sorry. I was thinking of..."

"Mmhmm." The brunette shot me a knowing look that morphed into a wide smile. "I'll bet you were. I know what that look means." She leaned closer to me as we continued shoulder-to-shoulder down the corridor. "I've also heard that your fighter is pretty hot—if you don't mind horns and a tail."

"I don't," I said, quicker than I'd intended. I guess I felt defensive of the Taori since so many on the battle moon had referred to him as a beast. He might have a few predatory features, but he was farther from a beast than almost any male I'd met. Even when he was consumed by the primal carnal fever, he was less of a beast than the monsters who ran the moon or watched the fights.

Kensie nodded, her smile slipping slightly. We rounded a corner, and she peered up and down the light filled corridor before touching a hand to my arm. "Be careful."

A twinge of irritation flared within me, and I stopped walking. "Don't worry. Naz would never hurt me."

Her smile turned down. "It isn't him I'm warning you about. I know what it's like to become attached to one of your fighters—and then lose him." Pain flickered across her face. "One of the first fighters I attended was a human. Not many human males end up here, because they usually aren't strong enough to defeat the alien creatures the Xulonians like to throw in the arena, but this guy was a trained space marine." Her smile became wistful. "He won for a while and attending him was like living out some kind of fantasy. He treated me more like a girlfriend than a servant, and it didn't take long for me to fall hard for him."

I waited for her to continue telling the story, but she was quiet, her eyes downcast. A lump formed in my throat as I could imagine all too well how the fantasy had ended. "He was finally defeated?"

Kensie inhaled deeply and lifted her head, squaring her shoulders. "They all are. That's how the games are designed. No one wins forever. They make sure of that."

I couldn't pat the woman's shoulder in comfort since I was holding a tray, but I tried to convey my sympathy with my eyes. "I'm really sorry. This is all so unfair and cruel."

She pressed her lips together so hard they went white then she forced herself to smile. "That's why I'm warning you. I don't want you to be as heartbroken as I was." Her smile became artificially bright. "Now I do my job and don't get attached, and it's better for everyone that way. Trust me."

I did trust her. There was no faking the pain that had contorted her face and clouded her eyes, but I also knew that my growing feelings for Naz weren't something I could turn off at will. That meant that it was even more crucial that we escaped before anything happened to him. The idea of being like all the other female attendants who would spend their lives seeing fighter after fighter be sacrificed to the entertainment of the Xulonians made my blood boil. It was almost as cruel a torture as being one of the fighters led to slaughter.

"Thank you," I said, returning the woman's smile. "And thanks for looking out for me."

She twitched one shoulder and started walking again. "Girls have to stick together, right?"

I fell in step with her, hating the fact that I was planning to leave the moon and leave all the other females behind. But not for long. Naz had vowed to destroy the twisted Xulonian moons, and I had no doubt that he and his reunited crew would do just that. Then we could liberate all the females in the arena complex and the captive fighters.

First, we had to find a way out.

CHAPTER
TWENTY-FOUR

Naz

I rolled over on my arm, cringing from the twinge of pain that reminded me of the gash and the fighter who'd given it to me. Muddled flashes of the match—pain, blood, screams—spiraled through my brain, but I brushed them away, instead, choosing to dwell on what had come after. I inhaled the spicy aroma of the water in the pool that we'd dripped all over the sheets, the scent filling my mind with images that were much more pleasant. My pulse leaped and my cock thickened in response.

"Tyrria," I moaned, reaching out for her in bed. I was eager to make as many memories with her in bed as I could, especially since we would probably be forced into the ring again soon.

When my hand closed over nothing but air, the spot she'd been on warm but empty, I sat bolt upright in bed. I scanned the entire room, my arousal quickly shifting to panic when I realized she was gone.

"Steady," I told myself. "She would not have left you alone." Knowing that didn't calm me. The possibility that she'd been taken sent a cold shiver of terror through me.

I might be a battle-seasoned kalesh of the Taori, but the mere thought of Tyrria being in danger made my body go rigid. I could easily face bloody battles and the threat of death, but I couldn't take the idea of her being hurt.

My gaze caught on the round table that usually held steaming plates of food and glittering glass carafes of wine. It was empty. Even the tray that Tyrria used to carry dishes on was gone. I released a sigh. She was probably fetching breakfast for us. That was the job the aliens had given her, after all. I might not expect her to serve me, but our captors did.

I raked a hand roughly through my hair, relieved that Tyrria was only in the arena kitchens, but livid with myself for being so easily frightened. I was kalesh. I flew boldly into battle. I did not scare easily. Until *her*.

This is why we don't have females on our sky ships, I reminded myself darkly. This is why we ride into battle untethered.

I'd crossed galaxy after galaxy in pursuit of the Sythian swarm, and I'd managed to avoid emotional entanglements. We'd never stopped for longer than it took us to resupply or gather intelligence about the path of the swarm, which had made it easier to avoid excess contact with others. Even my bouts of the Quaibyn had been handled without me forming a connection to the pleasurers who'd done me the service of burning off my fever. But Tyrria...

My throat tightened as I thought of the female with pink hair who'd been betrayed by everyone in her life. She'd managed to touch a place deep in my soul that I'd almost forgotten existed, the pain inflicted by her father causing a familiar ache. I growled at the raw emotion that throbbed like an exposed nerve. I would do anything to keep her safe, which made me weak—

and it put her in danger.

"My soul is hers until it crosses into the shadowland," I whispered, feeling the power of the Taori mating language, and the fear that it would be my undoing. I needed to moderate my feelings for the female, or my entire mission—and any chance of saving her—might be ruined. My goal had not altered, even if my heart now was held by another. I still had to escape and locate my crew—as many as had survived—and reunite us on our original mission.

I got out of bed and walked naked to the standing wardrobe, retrieving a pair of soft black pants that clung to my form without being tight. I pulled them on and strode to the door, heaving it open and almost smiling when the two drowsy guards jerked back and spun around.

"Where is my female?" I barked, intentionally omitting her name and making them think I was every bit the beast they believe me to be.

"Fetching you food," one of the tusked aliens said, swinging his baton in front of him. "Get back inside."

I grunted and slammed the door before allowing my shoulders to sag. She was safe—for now. "As long as I keep winning."

I hadn't allowed myself to linger too long on the battles I was being forced to wage against innocent aliens who'd been brought to the moon against their will. I'd been thrown into the untenable situation without any time to think about it, and with my Quaibyn raging inside me. Now that I'd burned off the fever with Tyrria and been locked to her in the mating clench, the Quaibyn should no longer rage like an inferno and turn me into an uncontrollable predator.

I gulped. As much as I'd needed to cure the fever in order not to go mad, the heightened strength and speed had given me an advantage in the battle ring. Without the fever, I would still be a fearsome Taori warrior, but I would be less deadly.

"There's not much time left," I said to myself. Without the fever driving me to protect Tyrria and mutilate anyone who got in my way, I would soon meet an opponent I could not defeat.

The door swung open and Tyrria strode in, coming to a stop when she almost ran into me. "You're awake."

I took a few steps back to allow her to enter and the door to close behind her. She walked briskly to the center table and set down the tray of filled carafes and two domed plates.

"We have to get the hell out of here," she said as she pivoted to face me.

My mouth had been open to say the same thing, but I was surprised by the intensity of her words. "Why do you say this?" I gave her a swift once-over. "Did anything happen to you?"

She shook her head, smoothing her sideswept bangs to one side. "No, but staying here isn't an option. It doesn't matter how strong you are or how much the crowd loves you now. The Xulonians will kill you eventually." She met my eyes. "They'll use other fighters to do it, but no one survives this place."

I didn't tell her that my chances were even lower now that the mating fever no longer burned within me. I wouldn't have traded anything for being with her, even if it meant I'd lost my primal strength and senses.

"I've been checking out the arena complex on my way to and from the kitchens," she continued. "It's a bit weird that there aren't obvious doors leading outside or any windows that look out, but there must be some ways to leave. All those spectators get here somehow, and the aliens who work here must leave occasionally."

"We were both brought here—you by a slaver ship, and me by creatures who discovered me after I crashed. There are ways in and out, even if they aren't easy to locate."

"Don't worry." Tyrria winked at me. "I'll find them. I do have free run of the place thanks to this baby." She tapped the hard steel of her collar. "No one seems to care where the attendants go, and from what the other women have said, we aren't being watched."

It hadn't occurred to me that we would be watched, and I instinctively cut my gaze around the room.

"According to Bobbie, each of the moons has their own 'thing' and they can't steal each other's thunder." Tyrria grimaced. "The lust moon is where all the occupants are watched. Here the Xulonians only watch the fights."

My stomach turned at the idea of being watched on a lust moon, and a possessive growl rumbled in my chest. My heart pounded, and angry heat burned my flesh. I would rip their eyes out before I would allow the red-skinned creatures to watch me with Tyrria. Maybe the Quaibyn hadn't completely abandoned me, after all.

Tyrria came up to me, placing her palms on my bare chest and leaning close. "You know what that means, don't you?" She gave me a mischievous grin. "They won't be able to watch us devise our brilliant escape plan."

I scooped her up in my arms and headed for the bed. "That is only one of the things they will not be able to watch us do."

CHAPTER
TWENTY-FIVE

Tyrria

I hummed as I walked down the corridor to the kitchens again, holding a tray of empty plates and carafes. The only reason I'd left the warm bed with Naz was because we'd polished off all the water and wine. If we wanted to continue to work up a thirst, I needed to replenish our drinks and our food.

Thoughts of the Taori's muscular body pinning me to the bed sent tingles down my spine and almost made me forget that we were both unwilling participants in the Xulonian's twisted battle arena. If I ignored the steel collar ringing my neck and the armed guards flanking all the doors to the fighters' quarters, I could pretend that we were living on a pleasure planet, where our only activities took place between the sheets.

The sight of two husky guards with scowls on their tusked

faces brought me back to reality, and I lowered my gaze as I passed the door, wondering for a moment which fighter was inside—and which female attendant. Even though my only interaction with the other captive females was in the kitchens, I felt a kinship with them. They'd helped me when I arrived and had given me snippets of information and advice when the guards and cooks weren't listening. Despite the fact that we attended different fighters who often faced each other, there was no competition between the attendants. We were all in the same situation, and there was an unspoken sisterhood that bonded us.

I rounded a curve in the hallway and stopped short. Shouldn't I be nearing the kitchens? Instead, I faced another long hallway. Instead of boasting a row of guarded doors, this corridor contained smaller doors and no guards.

"*Kushnit*," I said under my breath, the Kayling curse spilling naturally from my lips. As much as I wanted to forget about the culture that had rejected me, I couldn't shake all of it.

Turning on my heel, I started to walk in the direction from which I'd come. Then I hesitated. If these doors weren't guarded, that meant they didn't house fighters. I swiveled back to the long, empty passageway. What was behind these doors?

With a furtive glance over my shoulder, I walked on tiptoes along the shiny floors so my feet wouldn't announce me. The doors weren't as tall or wide as the ones that housed the fighters, and the spicy scent that clung in the air from the bathing pools wasn't present here. "These must not be residential quarters."

I still didn't have a good sense of the arena complex and how it functioned, aside from it seemingly being designed around housing and prepping the fighters. I'd heard dark whispers about the subterranean dungeons where new fighters were held until they proved themselves—or died trying—and

I'd seen both the arena itself and the kitchens staffed by alien cooks. But I had no idea where the staff slept, or how the operation was run.

A nervous shiver went down my spine. Had I stumbled onto alien barracks for all the other workers who didn't require guarding?

"This is a bad idea, Tyrria. You should not be here."

But why shouldn't I? I hadn't been told to stay away from certain parts of the complex. The point of the electrified collars was so they didn't need to monitor my movements. The attendants were allowed to move freely in order to fetch food and drink, and sometimes healing supplies for their fighters. Not that I suspected I could find any of that down this corridor. I'd been shown the supply station and the kitchens, and neither of those were down this hushed hallway.

Despite my fluttering pulse, I continued to the first door and leaned close to it. I heard nothing, so I held my breath, balanced my tray on one arm, and touched the flat button on the metal door itself.

It slid open silently. I braced myself for screams or for thick-necked guards to rush out with their batons raised. None of that happened. Nothing happened.

I released a breath and stepped inside the dimly lit room, my eyes adjusting to the lowered light. Since the rest of the complex was bathed in bright light, it was surprising to find a room that didn't have sun streaming in from skylights.

As my vision grew accustomed to the shadows, my confusion grew. I stood in a massive room that made Naz's suite look puny, but instead of being outfitted for living, it was filled from end to end with sealed pods of some kind. They were bullet-shaped and made of a matte, dark-gray composite.

I stepped closer to one of the waist-level pods and peered at the clear window in the lid. Then my heart lurched, and I almost dropped my tray as I jerked back. The crimson face inside wasn't looking at me, but the tight skin pulled over the sharp angles of the Xulonian's skull was still startling.

What was one of the aliens doing in a pod in what appeared to be a storage room? My heart pounded as I walked to another pod and peeked tentatively at the contents. Another Xulonian with eyes closed. They didn't look dead, but it seemed like an odd place to sleep, unless this was where the spectators came if they needed to rest between fights.

I shook my head. Would the aliens really make their valuable viewers rest in hard pods along with what appeared to be dozens of other Xulonians? That didn't make any sense.

Sharp rapping sounds outside the room made me freeze. Someone—more than one someone—was coming down the hall. I glanced desperately around the room for a place to hide. I might never have been prohibited from the hallway I'd wandered into, but I had a good feeling my presence would not be welcome.

I cringed at the thought of being shocked for snooping, remembering the burn marks I'd spotted on other attendants' necks. I did not want that.

I glanced down at my hands. Could I shift again like I'd done in the battle ring and partially in the corridor? I'd never successfully shifted at will. Not fully. The only time I'd effectively shifted had been when my life had been threatened. I didn't want to be discovered snooping *and* realize that I couldn't shift all the way. Even though my fingers tingled with the urge to try again, I shook my head.

Now isn't the time for a bad surprise, I told myself. Or to start leaving bodies to be discovered. Not when I could hide.

I hurried to the back of the room, being careful to walk on my toes and keep my tray steady, so the carafes wouldn't rattle even though my hands shook. Luckily, the back of the room was even more poorly lit than the front and there were some broken pods propped vertically against the wall. I flattened myself as close to them as possible, slinking into the shadows just as the door to the room slid open.

"How many did we lose last time?"

I recognized the guttural rasp of the guards as two of them lumbered inside.

"Two," the other said. "One malfunctioned and the other was due to be replaced anyway."

"Our dimensionals may not get as much wear and tear as the ones on the hunting moon, but we use so many more of them."

Dimensionals? What were dimensionals?

"That doesn't mean they're going to get us new ones. You know the director has been trying to get a new batch, but the directors on the other moons argue he has more to begin with."

I watched as one of the husky guards opened the lid of one of the pods, pulled out the Xulonians inside, and tossed him carelessly over his shoulder. Then he huffed out a breath. "The director is sure he doesn't want to repair this one?"

The other guard plucked a loose flap of red skin from the inert alien. "Too much damage. He's going to the incinerator."

My brain whirred as I tried to process what was happening. The body slung over the guard's shoulder wasn't alive or dead. Were the Xulonians in the arena actually cyborgs?

The guard holding the Xulonian or cyborg grimaced as he looked at the body flopping down his back. "Imagine being one of the red-skulls and having the chance to transfer your consciousness into another body—and you end up looking just like you always do."

"They don't even have tusks," the other guard said with a visible shudder as he yanked open another pod.

Transfer their consciousness? The Xulonians inhabited avatars?

"If they're too fearful to leave their planet, I doubt many of them are bold enough to try out a new body."

"They can transfer into other species on the lust moon, but from what I've heard there are only a few of the dimensionals that are other species." The guard pulled another limp Xulonian from a pod and tossed it over his shoulder. "I wouldn't mind going to one of the other moons."

"You know they don't use us on the other ones. We're lucky to be here."

"Lucky," one of the guards snorted. "If you call being stuck on a desert moon lucky. There's nothing on this ball of burning sand but the arena."

I swallowed hard. The rest of the moon was desert?

"Then be glad you're inside and not out on the sand dunes dying of thirst."

"At least we don't have to worry about escapes," the other guard let out a menacing laugh. "Even if they could find the tunnels, where would they go? There's nothing but sand and death out there."

"There's plenty of death in here. The director needs to pace out the fights more or we won't have anyone to fight."

"Another shipment is arriving soon, and from the transmission it sounds like they're bringing us another one like the beast. Imagine how packed the stands will be with two of them fighting against each other."

I stopped myself from sucking in a startled breath. Did they mean another fighter like Naz? Had they found another Taori?

"Then we'd better take care of these dimensionals and make sure the flight deck is ready for the delivery."

One of the guards opened the door and readjusted the

body on his shoulder. "How about we assign clearing the sand to someone else?"

I didn't hear the response as the door slid shut behind them, and I was left alone in the room. Well, aside from the pods filled with avatars.

A wave of revulsion passed through me as I eyed the rows of pods. The spectators cheering and jeering in the stands weren't even real. They were avatars being inhabited by Xulonians who were safe on their planet. Avatars who would cheer for blood as Naz was forced to fight against his own crew mate.

"Cowards," I hissed as I stumbled from the room and down the corridor, forgetting all about my trip to the kitchens.

CHAPTER
TWENTY-SIX

Naz

The hot water bubbled around me, tickling my nose as I let it wash over my shoulders and lap at my chin. I inhaled the spicy perfume of the water, the scent working to unwind the knots in my back even more. The water stung my arm less than it had earlier, which meant that the wound was healing, thanks to the properties in the water or whatever medicinal oils the aliens added. Or I was becoming numb to the pain.

It was hard to focus on pain when I'd been buried inside Tyrria, our limbs entwined and our bodies slick with sweat. The gashes on my body had been forgotten as our moans had mingled and our tongues had tangled. Even now, when I was alone in the pool and she was fetching more drink, my cock was rigid at the mere thought of the female.

It was better this way, I assured myself. I'd rather lose

myself in Tyrria than think about our fates. But despite how happy we were together, our situation and our future were more perilous than ever.

I pushed those dark thoughts from my mind. I was a Taori. A kalesh of the Taori. I would not be defeated so easily, and I would not allow any harm to come to my mate.

Mate. The word sent a jolt through me. Tyrria was my mate, even if she didn't know it yet. There was no other female for me, and the thought of any other male even glancing at her made my body flame with heat and my fingers curl into fists.

I closed my eyes and sank deeper into the water until I was completely submerged. My fists relaxed and my heartbeat slowed. I didn't have anything to fear when it came to Tyrria. She was mine, and I would fight to the death for her. The realization calmed my pulse as determination settled over me. For the first time in longer than I could remember, there was something more important to me than restoring my family's honor. My determination to find and save my Taori brothers had not lessened, but Tyrria was now part of the crew I was destined to save.

I stood and let the water stream from my body, swiping both hands across my face and down my hair, my fingers bumping the ridges on my horns. My calm was broken as Tyrria rushed into the room and set the tray down on the central table with a clatter. The empty carafes and plates were still empty.

Without a word, I leapt from the pool and strode to her, the water making a trail of puddles behind me. "What happened? Are you hurt?"

She shook her head. "I'm fine. Startled, but fine." Then her gaze traveled lower to my completely naked body, and the rock-hard cock jutting out so that it almost poked her. She glanced up and raised an eyebrow.

"If you're unhurt..." I said, leaning down to nuzzle her neck and sweet-talk her back into bed.

She took a step away. "I'm fine but I have to tell you what I discovered."

Her expression was so serious, my stomach tightened. "Discovered?"

"You sure you don't want to grab a towel?" Her cheeks were flushed as she averted her gaze from my cock. "That's a little distracting."

I quickly snatched a towel from the stack folded on a low side table and wrapped it around my waist. "I thought you went to the kitchens." I cut my gaze to the empty tray. "Was that not true?"

Her eyes flashed. "I was heading to the kitchens, but my mind wandered." She glanced at my tented towel. "Which was your fault, by the way."

"I am not the only one to blame." I glanced pointedly down at my towel. "You are a significant distraction."

Her cheeks reddened, and she pivoted away and exhaled loudly. "I must have taken a wrong turn, and I ended up in a hallway I'd never seen before. One with no guards flanking the doors."

"Not quarters for other fighters?"

She shook her head. "It was pretty deserted, so I decided to peek into one of the rooms."

I folded my arms across my chest. I did not like where this story was going. "That was an unnecessary risk."

"If we're going to find a way to escape, then we're both going to have to take some risks, and since you aren't allowed outside this room without armed guards, that means I need to be the one to do the recon."

Tyrria was right, but that didn't mean I had to like it. I grunted. "I cannot protect you out there. If you get caught—"

"I'll talk my way out of it. The guards already think females are brainless."

I frowned although I suspected she was right about the guards. "But you didn't get caught."

Another quick shake off her head. "I snuck into one of the rooms without being seen." She wrapped her arms around herself. "You know all the red-skinned Xulonians yelling and cheering in the stands?"

I gave her a single nod.

"They aren't real."

My frown deepened. "I don't understand."

"They call them dimensionals, but they're avatars. The Xulonians paying to watch the fights are back safe and sound on their home world—apparently they're too scared to leave the planet—but their consciousness is uploaded into avatars." Tyrria shivered. "I walked into a room filled with pods that held the lifeless avatars. Considering how many aliens are in the stands, I'm guessing the rooms on that hallway are filled with pods."

My stomach sank. "So, the Xulonians aren't transported to and from their planet." That explained why we hadn't been able to locate entrances and exits leading from the arena, but it also meant that the chances for us to escape had just dwindled.

Tyrria rocked back on her heels as she met my eyes. "I have more bad news. This moon is a giant desert with nothing but sand and this arena complex. If we escape from the building, there is no place to go where we could survive for long."

I flashed back to snatches of memories after I'd ejected from my sky ship and before I'd come to in the dank underground cell. There had been intense heat and blazing light. Had I crashed in the desert?

"How do you know all this?" I asked, my voice cracking as the disappointment hit me.

Tyrria dropped her gaze and shifted from one foot to the other. "A couple of guards came in, and I had to hide."

My jaw fell open. "You could have been discovered and—"

"But I wasn't," she said before I could remind her that the guards were very capable of inflicting lots of pain on her. "They were too busy complaining about their jobs and the moon to notice me."

My gaze flitted to her steel collar. I could withstand pain and injuries, but I could not endure seeing her hurt. The thought made my heart twist.

"If I hadn't been in that room, we wouldn't know that the spectators are only avatars or that the moon is all sand. This is good information to have as we plan our escape."

I folded my own arms over my chest, the idea of escaping feeling like a faint dream that was slipping through my fingers as I awoke. "If the Xulonians do not travel to the moon and there is nowhere to run to if we do escape the complex, our chances are slim."

"The Xulonians might not come and go, but they do deliver new fighters and new females. I was brought here by ship."

Tyrria was right. I might have crashed onto the moon, but the other alien fighters had to be abducted and transported by sky ship. That meant there was a flight deck somewhere near the arena. "Our escape must be tied to one of the deliveries of new fighters and females. And we must find the flight deck and learn the time of the next shipment."

Tyrria lifted her head and smiled. "I don't know exactly when the next flight will arrive, but I know that one is coming soon. I also know that the flight deck is close enough to the desert that they need to remove the sand before a ship arrives."

I pondered this for a moment. "So, it's probably not on the roof of the building."

"Especially since there are so many domes in this place."

Tyrria tipped her head to the glass dome over our heads that refracted colored light onto the floor. "But in a way, that means it will be easier to find. It has to be attached to the complex and close enough so the new fighters can be brought inside without being dragged through the upper hallways. I've never seen new fighters or attendants being brought in."

I pinned Tyrria with a forceful gaze. "You are not to search for the flight deck. It's too dangerous."

She walked toward me and rested a hand on my crossed arms. "What if I told you that the next shipment of fighters includes one of your Taori brothers?"

I drew in a sharp breath as my world tilted on its axis. Tyrria was right. This changed everything.

CHAPTER
TWENTY-SEVEN

Tyrria

His face went slack as soon as the words left my mouth. "One of my Taori brothers?"

There was such pain in his voice that my own throat tightened. "The guards said that there was another like you in the incoming shipment of fighters."

Naz scraped a hand through his damp hair, sending droplets of water to the floor. "They captured another of us? Did they say if he crashed on the moon as well, or if they snatched him from the sky?"

I shook my head. "They only said that another like you was coming." I didn't tell him that the monstrous guards had referred to him as a beast. I refused to repeat their cruelty, because I knew that Naz wasn't close to being a beast. He wasn't the one abducting innocent creatures and forcing them to battle to the death. Killing to stay alive didn't make him anything but a survivor.

Naz began to pace a small circle underneath the dome. "Who else could have made it to the surface of this moon? How long have they been in the desert alone before they were found?"

"Did all of your crew escape when your ship was destroyed?"

He looked up at me as if he was startled to see someone else in the room. "I was the last pod that left the ship, but I don't know how many reached the surface of the moon and how many were," his voice broke, "shot from the sky during their descent."

My heart ached for him, the turmoil inside him evident on his face. I took his hand and led him to the bed, sitting him on the edge and taking a seat beside him. "You said you wanted to reunite your crew, right? Well, it may only be one Taori, but at least this is a start."

He leaned forward, bracing his elbows on his knees. "You're right. I should be grateful that I will be reunited with one of my brothers."

I hesitated for a moment, considering if I should reveal everything to him. If the roles were reversed, I'd want to know. The thought of keeping important details from Naz didn't feel right, even if I knew the truth would rob him of his momentary happiness.

"I don't think we can count on your reunion being a good one."

He swiveled his head to me. "What do you mean?"

"These are the Xulonians. They're the kind of creatures who kidnap innocents and force them to be hunted or fight to the death or do who knows what on the lust moon, all so they can be entertained. They're cruel and twisted." I drew in a breath. "If there are two of you, they'll pit you against each other."

Naz recoiled as if I'd slapped him, his eyes widening. "Two Taori battling against each other?" Then he pressed his mouth into a hard line, as he shook his head and unleashed another torrent of water droplets. "I would never harm one of my warriors."

"That's why we have to use the arrival of these fighters—and your Taori crew mate—as an opportunity to escape. If we stay, they *will* force you to fight your fellow Taori."

Naz stood quickly, muttering darkly under his breath. The towel slung low around his waist slipped even lower. "That means we don't have long to find the flight deck and discover when the shipment of fighters arrives."

"Leave that to me," I said, even though I was obviously the only one of the two of us who had free access to the arena complex.

Naz glowered at me, although I knew he wasn't angry at me. "It's too dangerous."

I put my hands on my hips. "What's the alternative? Are you willing to fight your Taori brother to the death?"

"I am not." The way he said it made me certain that he would choose to sacrifice himself to keep the Taori he thought of as sons alive.

Fear sent chills down my arm. He might be willing to give his life for his Taori brothers, but I was not willing to give him up.

"Then you need to let me help you. Help us." I locked eyes with him. "I'm still holding you to your promise of getting me out of here, Kalesh."

His face contorted for a beat, but he walked to me, took my hands, and pulled me up so I was facing him. "A Taori never breaks a vow but—"

I held up a finger. I didn't want him to say out loud what I already knew. He could not kill one of his brothers—even for me. And I would not want him to be forced into that decision. As much fun as we'd had and as close as I felt to him, we still had only known each other for a short time. He'd been leading his crew for decades. They were his family, and he was the head of that family. I would never make him choose me.

"Let's leave it at that," I said. "You promised to escape with me, and I promised to trust you. Now, you're going to have to trust me, too."

"I do trust you." He squeezed my hands. "But *I* am supposed to protect you, and I can't do that when you leave this room."

"I'm more than I appear," I reminded him. "And I'm tougher than I look." I stared hard at my hands, willing them to shift.

When they morphed into pink, furry paws with long, curved claws, I cursed. Then I realized that my claws were as deadly as blades shooting out between my fingers.

Naz looked at my paws and glanced nervously at the door. "You should not let them know of your talent. It's too dangerous for them to know that *you're* dangerous."

I sighed, but knew he was right. I focused on my hands, and they shifted back to normal. My skill wasn't refined but there was no doubt I could now shift at will.

"You might have some natural defenses," Naz said, "but I cannot ask you—"

"You aren't asking me to do anything I don't want to do," I snapped before he could finish his sentence. "Do you really think I want to spend my life on this moon? Or even worse, do that without you?" I shook my head so hard my sideswept bangs flew around my face. "I'm doing this for both of us." I stepped away from him and strode to the table, picking up the tray again. "Now, I think it's time I go to the kitchens and see if anyone knows any gossip about the next transport. The guards were too busy arguing about something to notice the empty tray before, but this time I need to bring back food."

"I would not object to food."

I shot him a snarky look before I walked quickly from the room so I wouldn't lose my nerve and run back. What I'd said was true. I was doing this for both of us, but I was also doing it because I knew deep down I had to rely on myself more than anyone—even Naz.

It had been a lovely fantasy to imagine that the Taori could save me, but when it came down to it, the alien warrior couldn't abandon his brothers for me. He shouldn't. His mission hadn't changed, and neither had mine. He was returning to another life and another time—a time I couldn't imagine I'd fit into. As always, I would need to save myself.

CHAPTER
TWENTY-EIGHT

Tyrria

I ignored the guards as I left the room again, hoping they had truly been too distracted earlier. They didn't say anything or move from their posts, so I held my head high as I took deliberate steps toward the kitchens.

This time I'll pay attention, I told myself, as I focused on the correct twists and turns that would lead me to the wide door that announced its presence with clouds of savory steam even sooner than I spotted the door. I inhaled the humid, hot air billowing from the expansive space, my stomach rumbling at the combination of scents—charred meat, yeasty bread, crackling sugar.

The cooks clattered pans on the stovetops and chopped vegetables on well-worn cutting boards, but even over those sounds came the laughing of the other females. They were gathered at the beverage station refilling pitchers and carafes with their heads bent together and their giggles rising like the plumes of smoke from the ovens.

"Tyrria!"

I smiled when Kensie waved at me, her arm high in the air and her fingers flittering. I joined the group and set down my tray. "I'm not the only one late to get breakfast?"

"Breakfast?" Bobbie eyed me with a sly smile. "You have been distracted by your fighter. We're here for lunch."

My cheeks warmed but I tried to play it off. "Right. I guess I'm losing track of days and nights since the sun never seems to set around here."

"It's not like this all the time." Kensie held out a large bottle so I could refill my empty carafe. "There's a period where the only light comes from artificial lamps."

"But they keep those on nonstop then too." Bobbie tossed a blonde lock of hair off her shoulder. "They like things bright around here."

"Well, it is a desert moon," I said, dropping my first nugget of information and waiting for anyone to bite. "It makes sense that it would be sunny."

"How do you know that?" Kensie asked.

I shrugged. "I don't remember where I heard it. I thought it was common knowledge."

Kensie gave me a weak smile. "It is, I guess."

"No one talks about it," Bobbie said in a stage whisper, as she leaned in close to me. "I guess talking about the outside world makes it feel more real and scary."

A female with dark skin and braids arranged artfully on her head titled her head. "Being surrounded by a scorching desert is scary. I don't want to be thrown out into it."

My heart lurched. "That could happen?"

Kensie shot the woman a sharp look. "We have no proof that's happened, Trisha."

Trisha cocked an eyebrow. She clearly didn't agree. "Then where do they go when they disappear?"

"Who is *they*?" I asked, dropping my voice as some of the cooks shot our group sideways glances.

"Sometimes attendants vanish," Trisha said before Kensie could interrupt.

"Maybe they're taken off the moon," I suggested. "Do they ever disappear at the same time a new shipment of fighters arrives?"

Bobbie grabbed my arm and pulled me down, scanning the kitchens before lowering her head to mine. "Don't let anyone hear you talking about the arrival of new fighters. We aren't supposed to know about those."

"How do they think you don't notice new fighters?" I whispered.

Bobbie gave me a crooked grin. "You've seen the guards, right? Do they look clever to you?"

I couldn't help returning her smile. "So you all know but you have to pretend that you don't?"

"The key to surviving here is not to make waves," Kensie said, giving us all severe looks. "Don't let the guards think you know anything and don't step out of line."

That sounded like good advice if I wanted to stay here for the long haul, which I didn't. "Did the females who disappeared make waves?"

Pain flickered across Kensie's face. "Not everyone can handle the situation. I try to warn everyone." She gave me a pointed look. "Not everyone takes my advice."

Bobbie nudged me with her elbow. "Tyrria isn't making waves. She's attending the current champion. Why would she want to cause trouble? If she's smart, she'll ride that horse for as long as she can." The blonde winked at me. "In more ways than one."

I fought the flush that heated my face.

"We've heard your guy is unbeatable." Trisha looked up from arranging a pair of goblets on her tray. "And that you've been in the ring with him."

"Only because they forced me," I said, hoping that my shifting secret wasn't as common knowledge as everything else. "I don't know much about combat."

Kensie frowned. "They never should have put you in the battle ring. That's not part of the deal."

I wanted to remind her that we were prisoners and there wasn't any kind of deal, but maybe she stayed sane by convincing herself that there were rules and order in the arena. Maybe that was why she was so intent on no one making trouble.

"So far, Naz has protected me," I told them.

"The beast's name is Naz?" Bobbie shivered as she puckered her lips. "I like the sound of that."

Trisha rolled her eyes. "You like the sound of anything that has to do with a male."

"Not all males," Bobbie said, her own expression darkening for a beat. "You know I've had to attend some bad ones."

Kensie patted the woman's hand sympathetically, but I saw an opening.

"If you like the sound of Naz, I heard that another of his kind is arriving here soon."

All the female eyes swung to me.

"Another beast?" Trisha whispered.

I flinched at the word beast. Naz was the farthest thing from a beast I'd ever known, but I didn't want to get into a debate with them now. I wanted information, and I was convinced one of them had to know more than they were saying.

"How did you hear that?" Kensie said so softly I had to lip-read to decipher her question.

I twitched one shoulder and tried to appear nonchalant. "Maybe I overhead the guards talking about it." That was technically true.

Bobbie rubbed her hands together. "I hope I get assigned to him. I have a thing for barbarians. They're so deliciously rough."

"Don't you have a fighter?" Trisha asked.

Bobbie made a face. "After the wounds he suffered during the last fight, he won't make it through another."

"You'd better hope he fights again soon," Kensie said. "If Tyrria heard the guards talking about a new shipment, that means it's happening soon."

"Really?" I attempted to sound uninterested, even though my pulse quickened.

Kensie shifted from one foot to the other. "The guards rarely have much notice about incoming fighters. If they're talking about it, it's going to happen today."

"During the day?"

The brunette shook her head. "Shipments only get unloaded after the fights are over and everyone is in their quarters. I don't think they want us to inadvertently see the new fighters arriving as we're walking around."

"It's not like they'd parade the new captives through the upper halls," Trisha said. "New guys go straight below."

"The dungeons?" I asked, forgetting to lower my voice and getting a harsh look from Kensie.

"Don't call them that." She snuck a peek behind her, but the cooks seemed to be busily working and oblivious to our hushed conversation.

"Then the entrance to the flight deck must be underground," I whispered. "And the flight deck has to be attached to the arena complex somewhere."

Bobbie cocked her head at me. "Why all the questions?"

I waved a hand as if to dismiss her question. "No reason. I guess I was just a little curious when I heard the guards talking. You have to admit it's weird that there are no visible exits or entrances to this place."

"Because it's a fortress," Trisha muttered, lifting her tray and pinning me with her long-lashed, dark eyes. "It's not designed for anyone to leave. Not unless it's feet first. Don't forget that."

I swallowed hard as she sashayed away, her layered skirt swishing around her long legs.

Bobbie shook her head at the retreating woman. "Don't let her freak you out. This place isn't so bad as far as fortresses go."

One of the corpulent cooks lumbered over and slammed a massive pot on the counter near them.

"Stew again." Kensie sighed as she turned and began to ladle the steaming soup into a smaller tureen.

Bobbie pulled me closer while Kensie was distracted. "I don't know the location of any doors, but they bring in new fighters right beneath us." She pointed to the floor. "The sounds of the kitchens and the roaring of the furnaces in here mask the noise of the arriving ships."

I gaped at her. "How do you know this?"

She gave me a sly smile. "Sometimes I can't sleep, so I wander." Then she pulled her collar aside so I could get a better view of the scorch marks scarring her skin. "Insomnia has its dangers, though."

My mouth went dry as she readjusted her collar to cover her scars, but when Kensie turned around Bobbie was smiling brightly again. I picked up my tray and turned to leave, distracted by the information I'd learned.

"Aren't you going to take the beast some food?" Kensie asked.

I glanced at my tray, which only held one refilled carafe of wine.

Bobbie laughed, handing me the tureen she'd just filled. "Take this one, although with how dazed he's made you, I have a feeling you won't be eating."

I gratefully took the tureen of stew, trying not to read too much into the wink the blonde gave me before she resumed ladling the hot food, or the way Kensie had eyed me as I'd thanked them both and spun toward the door. I couldn't dwell too much on the females, when I had so much to tell Naz.

CHAPTER
TWENTY-NINE

Naz

My mind whirled with what Tyrria had told me as I sat at the long table with my elbows on the hard surface and my head in my hands. Another Taori was being brought to the battle moon? As much as I hated the thought of another member of my sky ship being a captive of the Xulonians, a part of me longed to see one of my fellow Immortals again.

The Ten Thousand were accustomed to living and fighting as one unit. We were not used to being scattered across the sky, and since I'd been separated from my brothers, I'd felt like I was missing parts of my own body. The ache of their loss was as palpable as the wounds now scarring my flesh.

Which of my crew was now being brought to the arena? My thoughts were muddled with names and faces tumbling through my head. I could remember the ink marking all of their bodies, from the sky chart etched on the back of our navigator to the enormous, screaming skull covering my first officer's chest. Which inked story would I see again when I was reunited with the Taori now in the arena complex?

Then my thoughts drifted to Tyrria. Despite her feminine appearance and her slight stature, the female was tougher than she appeared. I flashed back to her hands sprouting slashing blades that had torn into our opponent in the battle ring. She claimed she couldn't control the shifting and had never been able to do it at will, but she clearly possessed powers she didn't fully understand or embrace.

My heart thumped in my chest at the thought of training her to harness her powers and to fight by my side. She might not be Taori, but I knew she was the perfect mate for a kalesh. Thinking of her standing side by side with me on the command deck of a Taori sky ship sent hot pulses of pride and desire through me. Tyrria was as honorable and brave as any Immortal, and she deserved her place with me.

If she wished to take it, I reminded myself. I knew without a shadow of a doubt that Tyrria was meant to be mine, but I didn't know if she felt the same way. She came from a different culture and a different time. Was I delusional to think she would want to abandon everything she knew to return with me to the past? Did she even want to be the mate of a Taori kalesh? Would any female want to spend her life traveling across the sky with a sky ship full of Immortals and hunting down the Sythian swarm?

If I'd thought about it while our bodies were writhing together and slick with sweat, I would have said she wanted me as much as I did her. But now, alone in my quiet quarters, doubt crept in like dusky shadows.

"It matters not," I said aloud, the gruff timbre of my voice some comfort as it broke the silence. "We will escape together and then she can make her choice."

Even with my Taori brother arriving, my vow to Tyrria was unchanged. I was not leaving the alien moon without her.

The door swung open, and I leapt to my feet, expecting Tyrria to enter with her tray of food and drink. When it was not her, I tensed.

"Come with us," one of the guards said, his fleshy neck jiggling, as he tapped his baton against his leg.

"Another fight?" I cut my gaze to the towel still hanging around my waist.

The second guard shook his head. "No, but you should dress. The director won't want to talk to you like that."

The director? I stood still for another few beats, waiting for them to say more.

The first guard waved his baton at me. "Let's go, beast. The director doesn't like to wait."

I crossed to the standing wardrobe, dropping my towel as I walked and disregarding the presence of the guards. Taori didn't have any problem with nudity. Our bodies were one of the ways we expressed ourselves, and we took pride in the muscular form we worked hard to maintain.

Other species and planets hadn't always shared our comfort with exposed skin, and the sight of our dark markings had shocked more than a few aliens. I suspected these guards had seen plenty, and their comfort was the least of my concerns. I snatched dark pants and a loose, gray shirt from the cabinet, my gaze lingering on the rows of hanging outfits meant for Tyrria. As I pulled on my clothes, I wondered where she was, and what she would think if she returned to an empty room. Would I be returning to this place, or was this an excuse to remove and eliminate me without protest?

I spun to face them once I was clothed. "What about my attendant? Will she be told where I am?"

"Don't worry, beast. You'll be back before she is. You know how the females like to take their time."

That gave me some comfort. At least these guards believed I was coming back.

I followed the first guard out as the second one took up position behind me. For the briefest moment, I assessed the aliens and how quickly I would be able to disarm them. I had no doubt I could take them down, but without knowing where Tyrria was, it was pointless to attempt an escape now. Especially with my Taori brother en route. I would have to bide my time.

Our trio walked down the corridor, away from the entrance to the arena. We passed several doors flanked by guards who looked much like the ones leading me, and the aliens all grunted in acknowledgement of each other. I kept my head high and facing forward, even as I sensed the beady eyes following me.

We turned down a hallway without guards at the doors, and my escorts slowed their pace until we stopped at a set of double doors. The lead guard put his hand to a panel, which sounded a high-pitched beep.

The door opened, and the guards pushed me forward, shuffling in after me. I walked deliberately as I took in the room, which was less ornate than almost any space I'd seen in the complex, aside from the dank dungeons. Although there was plenty of bright light, the ceiling wasn't domed and there were no luxurious fabrics or decorative elements to the bare space.

The only thing that wasn't colorless and lacking interest was the creature standing behind the wide desk, his arms braced wide on the shiny surface and the hood of his cloak draped so that his face was obscured. Even so, bright red hands protruded from his belled sleeves, the bony fingers tapping rhythmically.

So, this was a Xulonian. This was one of the aliens who'd destroyed my sky ship and scattered my crew. My fingers tingled with the urge to lunge across the desk and snap his neck. I knew I could be quick enough so that neither of the burly guards could stop me before the alien was dead. But my thoughts returned to Tyrria. I couldn't risk her being punished for my actions.

I stopped across the desk from him and clasped my hands behind my back, waiting for him to tell me why he'd summoned me and to keep myself from leaping at him.

"We've never put an attendant in the arena before," he finally said, his voice hard and clipped.

I didn't respond since there wasn't a question.

The creature raised his head and flipped back his hood, revealing his sharp-boned face, with crimson skin stretched across it. I battled the urge to recoil but instead, I clenched my teeth.

"But your female seems to bring out the best fighting in you, and my viewers are clamoring for more." The Xulonian tilted his bald head at me. "But maybe you've grown too attached to her. Attachment can lead to weakness, and I'd hate for my prized fighting beast to have a weakness."

"I have no weakness," I snapped. I couldn't let them take Tyrria from me or separate us in any way.

He leaned forward and his mouth stretched into a smile that contained no warmth. "Not even for the female?"

"The female means nothing to me," I said, louder than I'd intended and forceful enough that both guards flinched. "She attends to my needs."

The Xulonian's top lip curled. "You defend her with impressive ferocity."

"She attends to me *very* well." I leered at him as if we were in on some cruel joke together. "I am as male as the next fighter. How do I know another female will be as skilled as her? If you wish me to continue to be your prized fighter, I suggest you do not alter what works for all of us."

The red-skinned creature entwined his spindly fingers in front of his chest. "As long as you don't forget who you're fighting for, beast."

I met his gaze, his cold, black eyes sending ice skittering across my flesh. "Understood."

There was no way I would ever forget who I was fighting for—my Taori brothers and Tyrria. Or who I was fighting against—the Xulonians and all who aided their twisted torture.

CHAPTER THIRTY

Tyrria

I hurried from the kitchens feeling triumphant. Now I had at least an idea of how to access the flight area, and a good sense that the shipment of new fighters would be imminent.

My mind buzzed with possibilities. When could I sneak out and explore beneath the kitchens? So far, the guards didn't seem suspicious of me, even when I'd returned from a food run without any food. I suspected they were bored and not too worried about frail females attempting to escape.

"Dumbasses," I muttered as I turned down a hallway.

It was true that the other female attendants didn't seem eager to stir up trouble, but I also got the sneaking suspicion that Bobbie wasn't as harmless as she seemed. I wasn't sure if I believed her story that she liked to wander at night. The scars on her neck seemed to be proof that she might have tried to look for a way out and gotten caught.

The thought of being shocked so hard that the collar burned my flesh gave me pause, but there was no gain without risk. Besides, Bobbie must have charmed her way out of any harsher punishment, which made me think that I could do the same. If a few scorch marks on my neck were the cost of searching for a way out, then so be it.

I stopped when I rounded another corner. I should have been on the corridor that held my quarters, but the hallway was unfamiliar. Had I been so busy considering options in my head that I'd gotten lost again?

I huffed out a breath and turned to retrace my steps. Then I stopped when I heard a familiar voice. What was Naz doing here? What was he doing away from our quarters?

I swiveled around and slowly moved toward the cracked door. One of the guards who usually stood outside our room was blocking the doorway, but he was also the reason it wasn't closed all the way. I flattened myself to the wall outside as I strained to listen. I could hear the Taori's voice, but I couldn't make out all his words. Who was he talking to, and what was this about? I was dying to crane my head around the corner and peek into the room, but I couldn't take that chance.

"Not even for the female?"

My skin went cold when I heard that voice. I'd heard that exact, clipped cadence when I'd been on the Hittite slaver ship. The holographic Xulonian had sounded exactly like this.

"The female means nothing to me," Naz boomed. "She attends to my needs."

I almost shrunk from the harshness of his words, and I squeezed the tray hard to keep it from shaking. I'd never heard the Taori speak with such cold disregard—and he was talking about me. The chill of fear that had sent bumps across my bare flesh now turned my heart to ice.

I'd only ever been with Naz when he'd been with me. I knew nothing of his interactions before we were paired together, or how he was when he wasn't around me—until now. Was this the real him? I wanted to believe it wasn't, but doubt crept into my mind like dark tendrils of curling smoke.

The kalesh had always told me that his mission was to escape and reunite his crew. Then he planned to destroy the Xulonians and return to his time. He'd promised to help me escape from the moon, but was that all part of some larger ploy? I was the one doing all the dirty work and finding the information to help with the escape. Had I been a fool to believe his promises? Was I merely a tool he was using to complete his mission?

"You defend her with impressive ferocity," the Xulonian said.

I held my breath, waiting for Naz to defend me like he had in the arena or say anything that sounded like the Taori I thought I knew.

"She attends to me *very* well."

I pressed my lips together so I wouldn't scream. The deep rumble in his voice would have normally sent heat pooling in my core, but now hearing him brag about the things we'd done —even if he wasn't overt—made hot bile rise in the back of my throat.

I forced myself to walk away on my toes so the guard at the door wouldn't hear me, and I kept my lips pressed together so fiercely that they hurt. When I turned the corner and hurried far enough down the hallway that I wouldn't be heard, I released a breath and doubled over. I managed not to retch all over the tray, but my hands shook as I attempted not to drop it.

I drew in gulps of air as I steadied my heart rate and

glanced around me. I couldn't lose it in the middle of the corridor.

"Come on, Tyrria." I coaxed myself to start walking again, even though my steps were wooden. "You've heard guys say worse about you."

I was no stranger to being talked about. It wasn't even the first time some male had bragged about me. But this was different, because I'd believed he'd been different. I'd allowed myself to believe that the kalesh truly cared about me.

He does, a small voice insisted, but a louder one echoed the words I'd heard him say to the Xulonian. *The female means nothing to me.* They were words I'd never have expected to come from Naz, and I hated that I could hear them so clearly repeating in my head.

My heart felt like it had been twisted into a knot inside my chest, but I managed to push through the pain and make it back to our quarters, even though I barely noticed the guards and attendants passing me. I stumbled into the room and set the tray onto the table with a clatter, barely registering that some of the stew sloshed over the side of the tureen.

I'd barely staggered to a chair and collapsed into it when the door opened, and Naz entered. His eyes met mine and concern creased his face, but before I could lash out at him like I so desperately wanted to do, the two guards with him stepped forward.

"Your meal will have to wait. You're required in the arena."

"Now?" My voice trembled. I was in no shape to go into a battle. Not when I wanted to kill the other member of my fighting team.

"Now," one of the guards barked, slapped his baton in one fat palm. "Unless you'd rather see what it feels like when attendants don't obey orders."

Naz swiveled his head toward the guard and growled, but I

was in no mood for his protective act. Not after I'd heard what he'd said.

"Fine," I snapped. "Let's go."

The Taori tried to catch my eyes as he changed into his battle shorts, but I kept my own gaze averted. When he took his place by my side, he tried again to get my attention. "Tyrria, what is wrong?"

My throat tightened and hot tears stung the backs of my eyelids, but I refused to cry because of him. After my father's betrayal, I'd promised myself I'd never cry over another male. I would not break *my* promise.

"You should not worry about me, beast," I said as we walked toward the arena. "You should worry about the fight and the fact that you have no more powers of the Quaibyn."

CHAPTER
THIRTY-ONE

Naz

I flinched when Tyrria called me a beast. It wasn't the word so much as the sharp edge of her voice, cutting into me like a finely honed blade being drawn across tender flesh. The guards in front and behind us prevented me from stopping her and demanding an explanation, but I searched my memory for what might have upset her. Had she learned something when she spoke to the other attendants in the kitchens? Or was she upset because she learned nothing?

The corridor leading down to the fighting arena was dark, with no domed skylights or windows streaming in light, and breathing deeply meant inhaling the dank, damp scents from the dungeons even further below—sweat, excrement, fear, death. I gritted my teeth as we passed a passageway that led to the cells where I'd been held, memories of the surrounding despair almost choking me.

"Tyrria." I reached for her hand even as she strode forward with her gaze focused on the broad back of the guard in the lead. She allowed me to take her smaller hand in mine for only a moment, before squeezing her eyes together as if she was in pain and wrenching her hand from my grasp.

"We should be thinking about the fight," she croaked out, the sharpness of her voice dulled and tinged with such pain that my heart constricted.

Before I could reply, we'd reached the gaping door leading into the bright arena. I was relieved to see light again, even though I was very aware what awaited us once we entered the ring. In the dim, stone passageway, the sounds of the crowd were muffled. Knowing that the spectators were not real Xulonians made it easier to block out their cries for blood that made the walls and ceiling tremble around us, and dust sift from the stones above.

"You two shouldn't have any trouble with this fighter." One of the guards in front turned and stretched his mouth into a malicious smile. "Which is why we gave him a blade."

"What?" Tyrria gasped and swung her head to me. "Our opponent is armed but we aren't?"

"Don't think your beast is ferocious enough to keep you from being gutted this time, girlie?"

Tyrria curled her hands into fists, and for a moment I wondered if she was considering whipping out blades of her own creation and slashing the guard's stomach open. I reached out and enclosed one of her fists in mine.

"It doesn't matter if he's armed," I growled, as much for Tyrria's benefit as the guards. "I will defeat him."

"Go on then." A guard behind us shoved me forward as the other guards stepped aside.

I stumbled into the arena, and Tyrria stumbled into me a second later. I caught her by the elbows to steady her, but she straightened and pulled away from me. My assurances had done nothing to restore her faith in me or douse her inexplicable anger.

Focus on the fight, I told myself as my Taori training kicked in, and I assumed a battle stance. I quickly scanned the wide, open space of the circular arena, blinking rapidly as my eyes adjusted from the low lighting to the blazing sun pouring in from above.

There he was. My gaze honed in on our opponent as he stood as far away from us as possible. I had to squint to assess him, but his nervous stance told me everything I needed to know. The fighter might be smaller than me and not built for battle, but it was his hunched shoulders and quivering blade that told me the fight wouldn't be long or challenging.

The other fighter wasn't a trained warrior, and my gut roiled at the thought of killing him. I'd never attacked opponents who weren't enemies out to harm my kind or other species. The Taori did not wage war against innocents. It had never been our way. We were fighters who battled for those who were too weak to defend themselves. We did not attack those weaker than us.

I slid my gaze to the stands, a wave of revulsion wracking my body as I watched the avatars shriek and wave their bony arms. The red skulls looked like monsters frothing at the mouth. They were the danger. Not the fighter who'd been forced into the battle ring with a blade he didn't even know how to hold properly.

For a moment, I considered leaping into the stands and ripping apart as many of the avatars as I could. I imagined tearing their fake bodies limb from limb and could almost hear the snapping of their bones and the crunch of their wide-eyed skulls beneath my fists. Then I remembered that the real enemies were safe on their planet and my cathartic rage would make no difference. I flicked a glance at Tyrria, who was still wearing the electrified collar. What would they do to her to stop my rampage?

"He's human," Tyrria said, her voice flat.

I pivoted my attention back to the fighter. I'd heard about humans from the Drexians we'd encountered—they took the females of the species as mates—but I'd seen precious few of them in person. From what the Drexians had said, humans hadn't achieved intergalactic space flight, and were limited in their exposure to other species and worlds. In this future, they must have overcome those hurdles.

"And this one ended up a captive on an alien battle moon," I said under my breath, despising the Xulonians even more.

"What?" Tyrria asked, but I only shook my head.

The crowd's screams were turning to jeers as the three of us stood on opposite sides of the arena unmoving.

Tyrria scowled up at the red faces. "Let's get this over with."

She started running toward the other fighter, her fists pumping. I took off after her, if only to ensure she didn't get hurt. The human male might be no match for me, but he was still larger than Tyrria. I caught up to her and we ran side by side toward the armed fighter. He crouched low, bracing himself for our onslaught, although I had no intention of attacking first.

Tyrria clearly hadn't decided that the fighter didn't deserve to be mercilessly killed like I had. When we reached him, she lashed out with a high kick. It fell short, but it did hit the tip of his blade, which wobbled.

She landed in a crouch, and I would have commended her fighting form if the human wasn't now advancing on us, slashing the long blade. We both ducked, and I yanked Tyrria to one side as the sharp edge sliced through the air over her head.

She jerked her arm from my grasp, shooting me a fierce look. "I don't need anyone fighting my battles for me."

I gawked at her for so long I almost missed the human lunging for me, the steel blade in his outstretched arm. I caught the blur of movement in my peripheral vision and instinctively dodged and then dove for the ground, rolled, and came up on all fours behind him.

He spun around to face me. Sweat ran down the man's face, and his eyes were wild. He knew he was outmatched, and that I was barely exerting any effort to avoid his attacks. How long could we fight like this without delivering a death blow?

With a desperate wail, he ran at me with the weapon over his head. I prepared to ward off his feeble attempt, but Tyrria flew at him from the side, knocking him to the ground and sending his blade skidding across the dirt floor.

I hunched over his inert form as the spectators roared their approval. He wasn't dead, only knocked out. As I was contemplating how to make the aliens believe he was dead, I felt the cold edge of the knife's blade at my throat.

"Don't move," Tyrria rasped.

The crowd went silent for a moment as the female held me at knifepoint, then they erupted in cheers so loud the ground shook under my feet.

I didn't turn my head, even though I could have easily disarmed her. "What are you doing?"

"You said I mean nothing," she choked out, her voice barely audible over the raucous crowd. "What do you say now that I hold your life in my hands?"

My heart hammered against my ribcage as everything fell into place. She'd heard me talking with the Xulonian director. I didn't know how. Maybe the twisted aliens had even arranged it for their amusement. But she clearly hadn't heard everything and didn't understand why I'd lied to them.

"You have held my life in your hands since the moment I met you, Tyrria."

The blade trembled, and I felt the sting as it nicked my neck. "You lied to me."

"No, I lied to them. I have never lied to you. My heart is as much yours as my life is. Neither of them mean anything to me, if you aren't by my side."

"How do I know you won't ditch me as soon as you get your crew back?" Her voice trembled as much as her hand. "That's what you truly want, right?"

"My duty as a kalesh is to protect my crew. It is a duty I take even more seriously because my father failed in his duty as kalesh when his ship was destroyed. My fear of repeating his legacy blinded me to the truth."

"What's the truth?"

"That you are as much a part of me now as my Taori brothers. My duty as a kalesh may be to lead and safeguard my crew, but my duty as a Taori male is to protect my mate."

Her breath hitched and her bottom lip quivered.

"You are my mate, Tyrria. I choose you. I will always choose you. I am bound by your eyes and to your heart. My soul is yours until it crosses into the shadowland."

I sensed her body uncoil and the cool of the blade pulled away slightly. I twisted to look up into her tear-filled eyes just in time to see them go wide, and her body jerk wildly, as her collar jolted electricity into her, and she crumpled to the ground.

CHAPTER
THIRTY-TWO

Tyrria

"Careful, you don't want to make it bleed any more than it already is."

"I'm being careful. Who knows more about taking care of burn wounds than I do?"

The furtive, worried whispers drifted to me like they were floating through the breeze. I didn't know who was talking or what they were talking about, but my mind was too muddled to worry about any of that. It was like I was cocooned in a warm haze of nothingness.

A biting pain on my neck jolted me from my fog. What the hell was that? I moaned and tried to lift a hand to swat away whatever was biting me, but my arm was as sluggish as my brain ,and I barely succeeded in raising my hand before it flopped back down.

"See? I told you."

"It has to be cleaned."

More whispers, but now the voices were clearer. I forced my eyes to open, blinking languidly up at a collection of concerned faces. The blurry faces swam into focus, and I recognized the females surrounding me. Then it all came rushing back to me—the alien battle moon, the arena, Naz. *Naz!*

I sat up so fast that the other attendants had to jerk back. "Where is he?"

Kensie put an arm around my shoulders and tried to coax me back into a reclining position. "You should rest. You got a serious shock."

Memory fragments flashed back to me. The last image I could recall was me holding a knife to the Taori's neck and watching a trickle of his blood roll down his throat. Why? Why would I do that?

I sank back and allowed Kensie to guide me onto the lounge chair. My head felt so heavy I could barely keep it upright, and after bolting up so quickly, my temples throbbed in pain. I gingerly lifted a hand to my head but paused when my fingers didn't bump the steel collar around my neck.

I held my breath as I brushed my fingertips across my now-bare throat. "It's gone."

"He tore it off you," Kensie said, stealing a brief look at the blonde standing behind her and holding a cloth that was splotched with red.

I let my fingers wander from the smooth skin until they touched something sticky. I flinched from the sudden pain. So, this was what they were talking about. I had cuts on my neck.

"Did I get cut by the blade?"

Kensie and Bobbie exchanged a look then Bobbie moved closer. "Don't you remember what happened?"

I tried to shake my head, but it hurt too much. "I remember holding the weapon to Naz's throat, but why would I do that?"

"Good question," Trisha muttered from where she stood behind Bobbie. "None of us saw it, but apparently you turned on him."

That didn't sound right, but my memories were slow to return. Snippets of conversation were teasing the corners of my mind, but they were so jumbled I couldn't make sense of them.

"I don't remember," I said, my voice breaking.

Bobbie knelt beside me. "That's what happens when you get a shock like the one those assholes gave you. Trust me, I've been there. It takes a while for your body and brain to feel normal again."

"Shock?" I closed my eyes for a beat, recalling profound pain that had torn through my body. Then it came together for me. "The collar. They shocked me with the collar."

"You're lucky they didn't blow your head off," Trisha said, gaining her a severe look from Bobbie.

"Not helping," Kensie said.

"Why?" I asked, hoping the other attendants had answers my mind couldn't seem to give me.

Bobbie blew a blonde curl from her eyes. "They said it was to stop you from killing your fighter."

"So, he didn't cut me?"

Kensie shook her head and dropped her eyes. "We didn't see it, but the guards said he didn't move when you held the blade to his throat. That's why they had to disable you. They were afraid you'd kill their prize fighter and he'd let you."

The bitter tang of bile rose in the back of my throat, but I forced myself to swallow both it and the feeling of horror that I'd actually tried to hurt Naz. Even worse was that he hadn't fought back. Not that I was surprised by that. My gut told me that he'd never hurt me.

Bobbie leaned in, dipped her cloth in a bowl of water, and

dabbed it tenderly on my neck. "Don't think of any of that now. You need to focus on healing."

I gritted my teeth as she applied some sort of salve to my wounds and then bandaged them. As she worked, I closed my eyes and opened my mind. The answers were there if only I could make sense of them.

The female means nothing to me.

Naz had said that, but when and why? Heat flushed my body as I heard his cold words in my head. Then I remembered being enraged by what he'd said, the shame of feeling betrayed by him compounding with a lifetime of betrayal by those who were supposed to care.

You have held my life in your hands since the moment I met you, Tyrria.

The Taori's voice again, but this time it was the deep, rumbling timbre I knew so well.

I have never lied to you. My heart is as much yours as my life is. Neither of them mean anything to me, if you aren't by my side.

Then I was back in the arena holding the steel to his neck and watching a drop of scarlet blood trickle down his bronze skin. I'd pulled back the blade and he'd twisted his head to meet my gaze, his iridescent blue eyes shining. I'd seen then that he was telling the truth. All my fears about him had been just that—my fears. They had nothing to do with him. He'd done everything to protect me.

My pulse spiked as I opened my eyes to see Bobbie sit back and nod appreciatively at her work. "That should help."

"Where is he?" I asked.

"Your fighter?" Kensie's brow furrowed as she glanced at the other women. "We don't know."

For the first time since I'd regained consciousness, I scanned the room. It wasn't my room. It was the room I'd originally woken in, the room for the attendants when they weren't with a fighter. "Why am I here? I should be with Naz."

"Well, you tried to kill him," Trisha said, but her voice wasn't unkind. "And you needed a healer."

Bobbie gave a half shrug. "And I'm the closest thing we've got."

It occurred to me that even before I'd held the Taori at knife point we'd been engaged in a battle with a human opponent. "What about the fight? All the fights here are to the death. Who won?"

Kensie put a hand on my arm. "We don't know. All we know is what we overheard the guards saying, and they didn't mention what happened to the other fighter, or your guy, after you were shocked."

Panic threatened to choke me, and I managed to stand without swaying. "I need to go to our quarters. I need to find him and explain." My throat tightened with emotion. "I need to tell him I'm sorry."

"If the guy was going to let you slit his throat, I don't think he needs an explanation." Trisha put her hands on her hips and cocked one hip. "He's clearly in love with you. Not that it wouldn't hurt to apologize for going all she-beast on him."

The idea of being a she-beast made a laugh spill from my lips. Maybe that's what I was, the counterpart to his beast persona. I didn't care what I was, or what anyone wanted to call me, as long as I could be reunited with Naz and tell him that my heart was his as much as his was mine. "I still have to find him."

Kensie met my determined gaze and gave me a single nod. "The guards won't want you wandering without a collar." When Bobbie opened her mouth to protest, Kensie barreled on. "Which is why we'll distract them while you slip out."

"Won't you get in trouble?" I asked, my gaze going to the collar around her neck.

"If there's anything to take a stand for, it's love." She smiled wider than I'd ever seen before. "Now go find your guy."

"If we're going to do this, I have an idea," Bobbie said, rubbing her hands together. "Play along, girls."

She pushed Kensie onto the lounge chair and grabbed my hand. She pulled me behind her until we were at the door, which she opened and then immediately started shrieking. "What were you thinking by shocking another one of us? I think she's dead!"

The guards rushed into the room, goggling at each other and Kensie lying prone with her head flopping to one side. Trisha started sobbing loudly and threw herself over the woman so her neck wasn't easily visible.

With a wink, Bobbie shoved me out the open door. I mouthed 'thank you' as I ran from the room and down the hall. I held my arms by my side, but my hands tingled with the desire to morph into something deadly. When there were no guards posted at the doors I recognized to be mine, I thanked the old gods that I hadn't been forced into violence.

It was only when I hurried inside and eagerly scanned the luxurious room for the Taori that I realized what the absence of guards meant. Naz was gone.

CHAPTER THIRTY-THREE

Naz

"Where are you taking me?" I struggled against the guards as they shackled my ankles and wrists with the same type of irons I'd worn when I first arrived.

After Tyrria had collapsed onto the dirt, I'd leapt to her aid, calling her name, and stroking her face as she lay limp in my arms. I'd been aware of the guards running from both entrances to the arena, but even their heavy footsteps hadn't been noticeable compared to the thundering roar of the spectators.

Instead of being horrified that Tyrria had held a blade to my throat, they'd gone wild for it and cheered for her to end me even as I was telling her the truth and confessing that my life was nothing without her. I'd only lied to the Xulonians to save her.

I'd spoken the truth, even though it would also save my life. I didn't care about a life without her. Holding her body and feeling the slow, thready beating of her heart and the faint breath slipping from her lips, I didn't care about anything but keeping her alive.

Blood dripped from the scorch marks around her neck, and I used both of my hands to pull at the steel collar. The hard metal bit into my hands, but I only bellowed louder as I tore it apart and threw the pieces aside.

"Tyrria," I pleaded, bending my head so I could whisper in her ears over the screeching crowd. "Death might whisper at you from the shadowland, but this is not your time. Our fate was written in the stars, and it does not end now."

She made a soft, incoherent noise that made my heart soar, but before I could coax her awake, I was jerked up and she was wrested from my grasp. As hard as I'd fought against being taken from her, the guards had stunned me with their batons until I lay quivering and shaking on the ground. Memories of being dragged from the arena to a mixture of cheers and boos were vague. When I'd regained consciousness, I was being held by six thick-necked guards as they secured me with ankle and wrist chains.

"You're going back to the cells," one of the guards sat as he spat at the floor. "Director's orders. He thinks the girl made you soft."

I growled at this, lunging for him but being snapped back by the heavy chains. There was little I could say in argument. The entire arena had watched me do nothing as Tyrria had held me at knifepoint. If she'd truly meant nothing to me, as I'd claimed, I would have disarmed her. If I'd wanted to remain the champion and please the crowd, I would have killed the human and then the female.

The guards slammed heavy palms into my back to force me to shuffle forward. My nose twitched as I was hit with the pungent aromas I remembered from before, the dank cold enveloping me as we moved farther down the dark corridor. Moans, and the rattling of chains, grew louder as we descended farther underground, along with a sinking feeling in the pit of my stomach.

I'd broken the rules of the battle moon. I doubted I would be returned to fight again now that I'd shown my weakness. I wondered if I was being taken to a cell again, or if I was being taken to be tossed into the desert that surrounded the arena. Not that it mattered. Now that I'd been separated from Tyrria, all that mattered was finding her and escaping.

If she still wanted me. I thought about the look in her eyes the moment before she'd been shocked. Had she believed me? Had she realized that I would never lie to her, and that I didn't think of her as someone to be used and discarded? Or was it too late?

I cursed myself for ever uttering the lies I had to the Xulonian. Even though I'd done it to keep Tyrria safe, I'd caused her pain. The thought of her hearing me speak so dismissively of her made my stomach harden into a tight ball. I despised the words that I'd felt compelled to say almost as much as I hated myself.

When we reached the end of a corridor that was so dimly lit I could barely see my own feet moving on the ground, one of the guards swung open a creaky metal door of bars while another unfastened my ankle and wrist shackles. They gave me a hard shove so that I stumbled inside the cell. My leg muscles were still weak from being beaten and electrocuted, so I fell to my knees, groaning at the sudden pain.

"Maybe being down here will toughen you up." A guard slammed the bars shut and they all lumbered away, laughing roughly.

I pushed myself up, gripping the cold bars and leaning my forehead against them. Maybe all wasn't lost. I was still inside the arena complex. Now, I needed to find Tyrria and discover the way out. I pushed aside any thoughts that she might not have survived, telling myself that my mate was alive, and I would find her.

"Into the valley of death ride the Ten Thousand," I whispered, to give myself strength. If I'd been standing on the command deck of my ship, my Taori brothers would have bellowed the response, and our voices would swell until they echoed into our bones.

"We are the Taori," a voice rasped from deep within the shadows.

My heart stuttered in my chest as I said with him in unison, "We are the Immortals."

CHAPTER
THIRTY-FOUR

Tyrria

My stomach churned as I stood in the empty room, breathing in the spicy scent of the bubbling water in the sunken pool that reminded me of Naz, and trying to tear my gaze from the rumpled sheets on the bed that stirred up memories that now caused me as much pain as pleasure. Had I ruined things for good by letting my fear overpower my faith in the Taori?

It was clear that by spoiling the Xulonian's fight and turning on Naz, I'd broken the rules. They wanted battles to the death, and he'd refused to fight back and take me out. Did that mean he'd been forced to finish the fight against the human? Was it possible he'd lost?

I shook my head, forcing that thought from my mind. Impossible. Even without the added strength of his mating fever, Naz was quicker and more skilled than his opponent. Then why hadn't he been returned to his quarters?

The sick feeling in my gut intensified when I remembered what the other attendants had whispered about. The Xulonians wouldn't have put him out onto the punishing desert terrain of the moon, would they? Was Naz being tormented for my weakness? Had he already paid the ultimate price with his life?

"I have to find him," I said to myself, refusing to allow myself to dwell on the possibility that the Taori might already be dead. If I believed that, I wouldn't be able to move—and I had to keep moving. The other females had given me a head start, but soon, I'd be missed, and the guards would come for me.

I touched a hand to the bandages around my neck. For now, I wasn't controlled by their cruel collars. If I wanted to keep it that way, I couldn't waste time thinking the worst. Fear had almost ruined things completely before. I refused to let it rule me again.

Striding from the room, I paused outside the door. I didn't know where Naz could be, but if he wasn't in the room he'd been given for being a champion, he must have been taken someplace to serve his penance. My instinct told me that was down.

I hurried along the corridor, grateful that there were no guards as I headed toward the dark passageways that made Naz flinch when we'd passed them on the way to the arena. I didn't have to be empathic to know that those corridors led to places much less pleasant than the bright upper levels of the arena complex.

Most of the dizziness and fatigue I'd experienced after being electrocuted had passed, but I was sure that was because adrenaline was coursing through my system. I was alert not because my body had fully recovered from the trauma, but because I had to be. Naz was in trouble because of me, and I had to make it right. My body tingled with anticipation and my pulse fluttered like a trapped bird as I made my way as stealthily as possible down the narrowing hallways that sloped down.

I smelled the subterranean corridors before I saw them, the scent of dampness wafting up along with cooler air that prickled my bare skin. I hesitated before I descended further. Should I try to shift now? My experience shifting was so limited that I didn't know how long I could maintain another form. Every other shift had been brief, but was it possible to hold another form for a longer period of time?

Like so many times in my life, I wished with all my heart that my mother was around to help me. She would know the answers to my questions. Regret was a deep ache that throbbed in my body like an ancient wound, reopening fresh and sharp when I least expected it. If only my mother had lived long enough to teach me what it was to be a Lycithian, I thought for the millionth time. She could have told me about my heritage and nurtured my talent, instead of forcing me to suppress it. She would have been proud of my abilities, not ashamed. But I'd learned long ago that wishing didn't bring her back.

"Maybe she isn't entirely gone," I whispered, flicking my fingers through my hair. I had her pale-pink hair, and now I'd discovered that I'd inherited her abilities to shift. My mother lived on in me more than I'd ever thought, which might be why my father had looked pained every time he'd looked at me. Was I a reminder of what he'd lost, too? Would it have been too much for him to nurture her qualities in me, even if he'd known how?

I wasn't ready to forgive him. Maybe I never would be. But I was ready to harness my mother's strength to save myself and Naz.

Closing my eyes, I drew in a deep breath and focused on my scant memories of my mother—the way she brushed her long, pink hair from her face, her easy smile, her love of animals, which we'd had in abundance when she'd been alive. I didn't have any memories of her shifting, and I'd always assumed my father had forbidden it. I did remember cuddling with my mother's large, fluffy cat as I'd fallen asleep each night, the purring lulling me to sleep. When my mother had died, the cat had vanished, adding to my heartbreak and loneliness and giving me one more reason to despise my father.

For the first time, the truth about the cat I'd fallen asleep with hit me like a brick. I hadn't thought about her in ages, but now the memory of the pale pink fur on the tips of its ears and paws, and that stark realization, were like a message. I concentrated all my energy on my memories of the cat that had been my mother, my arms and legs buzzing with energy, and my heart racing.

When I opened my eyes, I no longer stood on two feet. I was much lower to the ground, and my hands and feet were pink-tipped paws. I would have cheered if I could speak, but instead I padded briskly down deeper into the shadowy corridors.

My vision wasn't impeded by the darkness, and I could easily navigate the winding, stone passageways and even skirt by a pair of guards lolling on chairs, with their heads tipped back. My new form might not be ferocious, but it made it possible for me to pass unnoticed into the dark underground collection of cells fronted with heavy, iron bars.

I moved noiselessly down a long passageway, glancing from side to side and peering inside the dank, fetid cells.

Bodies hunched over in the corners or curled on hard benches, silent as only rodents scurried across the slick, stone floors.

Turning a corner, I heard the hum of low voices at the far end. I ran quickly, the dark masking my approach.

"Is it truly you, Kalesh?" one of the voices asked.

"It is."

My heart leapt when I heard Naz's response. I'd found him, and it seemed that he'd found the other Taori.

Both warriors were standing at the bars of their cells, their hands curled around the cold iron as they leaned their faces between the hard, unyielding rungs. I could see what they couldn't in the dark. They were both wounded and marred, with blood over their darkly inked skin, their long hair was matted, and their tails hung limply behind them.

I slid through the bar into Naz's cell, rubbing against his leg and purring with happiness that I'd found him. I didn't know how I was going to free him, but at least we were together again.

He jumped and kicked out at me, almost landing a blow on my side, but I nimbly dodged him.

"You're lucky I have the reflexes of a cat," I said. "That would have hurt."

"Tyrria?" Naz staggered back, but I could no longer see him clearly.

I'd shifted back into my permanent form, and pushed myself from the floor, wiping my dirty hands on the front of my bare thighs. Interesting. When I'd shifted, my clothes had fallen loosely from my smaller, cat body, and now that I'd shifted back, I was naked.

"You didn't think I'd leave you to have all the fun, did you?" I asked.

"I didn't..." His words trailed off. He hadn't known if I still believed he'd betrayed me. The last time he'd seen me, I had been holding a blade to his throat.

"Know if I was still filled with murderous rage?" I finished for him.

"Or if you were alive." He reached out for me in the dark, his voice thick.

I released a heavy breath as I fell into his arms. "We're both alive."

"How did you find me? How did you get into my cell?" His hands moved down my back, and he stiffened as he clearly realized I was unclothed. "Why aren't you wearing anything?"

"That's a lot of questions." I leaned my face against the comforting firmness of his chest. "First, why don't you introduce me to your Taori crew mate?"

"I am Kaos, the first mate to Kalesh Naz," the Taori in the other cell said.

"This is Tyrria," Naz said, stroking a hand down the back of my hair.

Before he could explain who I was, a guttural laugh echoed down the row of cells. "It sounds like the beasts are ready to prove their worth in the battle ring. Our viewers have been eager to see two beasts fight."

"We don't even need to fetch the female," another snorted. "And did I hear that she's unclothed? The spectators will love it when we throw her naked in the arena."

Despite the warmth of Naz's arms that tightened around me, cold fear slid down my spine.

CHAPTER
THIRTY-FIVE

Naz

I was pleased to see Tyrria and know that she was safe, but that didn't lessen my confusion as to how she'd found me, or how she'd snuck into my cell without me knowing. Had she been there when I'd been shoved inside? I hadn't seen her since they pulled me away from her in the arena, but she'd barely showed signs of life as she'd sagged in my arms. Now she was standing by me and seemed to be healed.

It was too dark to see her well, but her voice was strong, and she was standing on her own. At least she was now. When I'd almost kicked her she'd been on the ground. And why was she naked? I couldn't imagine her traipsing through the arena complex unclothed and making it all the way down to the cold dungeons without being accosted.

She stiffened beside me as the guards plodded toward us,

and my mind raced. How was I going to protect her now? And what about my first officer? Did they truly intend to force us to fight each other?

"What does he mean?" Kaos asked.

I'd forgotten that he was new to the arena. I hadn't understood the level of the Xulonian depravity and cruelty until another captive had explained it to me.

"This is a battle moon, devised by the aliens who attacked us unprovoked and destroyed our ship. They abduct aliens and force them to fight each other to the death while their citizens pay to watch."

"Avatars of their citizens," Tyrria corrected. "They aren't brave enough to leave their home world. The cowards entertain themselves while inhabiting avatars."

Heavy breathing was Kaos's only response until he grunted roughly. "I assume our plan is to destroy them and stop their brutal practices."

I smiled at my first officer through the dark, my eyes making out the shape of him as he stood facing me, his tail swishing behind him and his silvery horns catching the only sliver of light. "You assume correctly. Our fate and theirs were written in the stars."

"And our fate is to destroy them like we've destroyed so many enemies before."

I let my deep growl join Kaos's. I didn't know how we would be victorious, but it was as inevitable as the rising of the sun over the mountains of Taor.

As the guards reached our cells and pressed their hands to a device on the door to open them, Tyrria pulled away from me. Was she attempting to hide from them, or delay being taken from my cell?

I reached for her, but my hand closed over air. I squinted through the shadows, hoping to see her willowy form, but instead I heard the predatory rumble of an animal moments before it sprang forward. The guards screamed as the creature leapt onto them, gnashing at flesh and sending them falling to the ground. The shrieks soon faded as the guards were silenced, and the creature straightened and changed shape.

"Let's go," Tyrria said from where she stood over the dead guards.

I walked forward, still not sure what had happened while Tyrria handed me a bloody stump of a hand. "You're a…"

"Lycithian shape-shifter. I guess I'm more Lycithian than I thought I was."

I thought back to the flash of blades that had emerged from her hands in the battle ring. "Your hands in the arena."

"That was the first time in a long time, but now I'm learning to control it."

"That's how you got into my cell."

"And why I'm currently not wearing any clothes."

I glanced down at the torn hand from one of the guards. I might not be able to see it clearly, but I could feel the blood dripping onto my own hand.

"For releasing the rest of the poisoners," Tyrria said, snatching her own dismembered hand from the floor.

I made my way to Kaos's cell, expecting to find it closed, but it hung open. I swiveled my gaze and spotted him still clenching the iron bars. "It's time to leave."

He hitched in a ragged breath. "I don't know if I can control it, Kalesh."

I instantly recognized the strain in his voice and the desperation to retain his sanity. The Quaibyn. "When did it start?"

"After I crashed. When I woke half-buried in the sand, I thought it was the brutal heat that was making my body feel like it was aflame, but it wasn't. It's the fever, and it's stronger than it's ever been."

"I was also afflicted. I share in your pain, brother."

He groaned. "You should go without me. I am too far gone. I can barely breathe in the scent of your female without wanting to pin her to the wall and claim her."

A possessive rumble shook my chest. As much as I honored my first officer and trusted him with my life, I would not let him touch Tyrria.

"I would never dishonor you, Kalesh," he gritted out. "You must leave me behind."

"To go insane?" I shook my head brusquely. "Never."

"Then kill me," he begged. "Please, Kalesh Naz. Do not let me pass into the shadowland in such dishonor."

"No one is killing anyone," Tyrria said. "Unless they're Xulonians or alien guards. We're all escaping together. Got it?"

Kaos twitched at her commanding voice, but he straightened. "I believe you have found a female worthy of a kalesh."

Warmth filled my chest, but I reminded myself that we were still standing in the cold, bleak dungeons, and we were far from free.

"I'm going to run ahead and find my clothes for all our sakes," Tyrria said, tossing her severed hand to Kaos. "You two handle the prisoner liberation."

I wasn't used to taking orders, especially from a female, but I didn't mind them from Tyrria. Especially since I knew she was mine to command in bed.

By then, there were restless murmurings from within the cells as the captives realized what was happening. We moved as swiftly as we could in the darkness, fumbling with the bloody stumps until we activated all the cell doors.

The aliens who'd been abducted to be fighters ran out as if they were insects scattering in the light, even though I shouted at them to stay together. I didn't blame them for their urge to run as far from the horrid subterranean prison as possible. I had to fight my own instinct to race behind them and rush for the light.

Still, Kaos and I worked in tandem releasing every prisoner as we made our way down the corridor. When we reached the end, my first officer nudged me and pointed to a barely noticeable alcove.

"That is where I entered this place."

I stared at the doorway that was shrouded in shadows, although hints of light were now trickling in as the floor sloped up . "This leads outside?"

He nodded, the silhouette of his face set in fierce intensity as his body trembled. It was obvious that keeping the fever at bay was taking all of his energy.

Tyrria ran up to us fully dressed, even if the clothing looked like it had been pulled on haphazardly. "Why did you stop?"

I inclined my head toward the arched doorway. "This is the way out."

She gasped. "You found it." She tilted her head up as if peering through the stone ceiling. "That makes sense. The kitchens should be right above us."

I didn't ask her why that was important, but she seemed pleased by the fact.

"When did you arrive?" she asked Kaos.

He blinked at her a few times as if attempting to process her question. "Not long ago. I'd barely been in my cell before they brought my kalesh."

"Did you arrive on a ship?"

He nodded. "I was put on a transport and brought here with others."

"So, the ship might still be here." Tyrria looked longingly at the door.

SUBDUE

I grabbed her hand. "Let's go find out."

She resisted my efforts to pull her forward. "I can't leave. Not without my friends."

The other female attendants. Of course, she would not want to leave them behind. They were just as innocent and deserving of freedom as we were. "Then let's hurry."

She smiled at me and led the way to the upper level of the complex. We sidestepped several more mutilated guards, and I reminded myself never to make Tyrria angry.

When we reached the bright hallway with light streaming in, I stopped and turned to my first officer. "You go with Tyrria and free the females. I have something I must do."

Tyrria opened her mouth to argue, but I swept her into my arms and silenced her questions with a hard kiss. When I released her, she looked pleasantly dazed.

"I will meet you at the exit," I told her before I locked eyes with Kaos, who gave me a tight-jawed nod. Then I ran in the other direction to settle a score.

CHAPTER
THIRTY-SIX

Tyrria

I didn't question Naz. I was aware of his list and those he needed to punish, although a part of me wished I could be with him. I itched to exact some vengeance, myself.

"Where are these female captives?" the other Taori asked, his voice husky.

Now that we'd emerged from the dark subterranean level of the complex, I took in Naz's crew mate. He'd introduced himself as the first officer to the kalesh, but he wasn't like any first officer I'd ever seen. Aside from being as tall and broad-shouldered as Naz, his chest was inked with the image of a giant screaming skull that ended in dark swirls stretching up his collar bone to his neck. His dark hair was long and caked with dirt, but a braid hung from one side. Like his leader, his eyes were a startling shade of blue that seemed to bore into me.

I snatched my gaze from the warrior's bare chest and tattered pants, waving a hand toward our destination. "Most of them should still be in the common room."

I hoped they were still there. The chance of invading the kitchens and escaping without being challenged was slim. I was already risking our odds of escaping by insisting on bringing as many of the females as we could find, but I knew that leaving them behind would haunt me.

Kaos gave a single nod as I hurried down the corridor, mentally preparing myself to shift if we encountered any guards. I released a breath when we reached the unmanned door. "In here."

I pushed open the door, ignoring the shocked faces as I rushed inside. Luckily, Kensie and Bobbie were still there, although the blonde lay outstretched on the lounger with a hand pressed to her cheek.

"Tyrria!" Kensie's gaze went from me to the Taori, her brow creasing in confusion. "Is this—?"

"It isn't Naz," I said impatiently. "It's his first officer, Kaos."

I cut a quick glance at the alien, who hadn't entered the large room. Instead, he stood in the doorway, with one hand braced on the frame and the other coiled into a white-knuckled fist. His breathing was ragged, and his face was flushed. Was the Quaibyn overtaking him?

I didn't have time to worry about the Taori. We needed to get the females out and get back to the exit before our movements and the Taoris absence from the cells was noticed. Once we were off the battle moon, we could deal with the mating fever issue.

"The other beast?" Bobbie sat up and dropped her hand from the bruise blooming on her cheekbone.

"What happened?" I stared at the red mark that was starting to show signs of purple.

She flapped a hand at me. "It's nothing."

Kensie shook her head. "The guard backhanded her after he realized we were faking, and you were gone."

"They know I'm on the loose?" So much for flying under the radar.

"They think you went back to your quarters with the..." Trisha flicked her gaze to Kaos then back to me, "...other guy."

"I did, but he wasn't there. They'd taken him underground." My stomach did an uncomfortable flip. If they looked for me there, they'd stumble over more than a few dead guards. I shook it off and squared my shoulders. Nothing I could do about that now. "Are you all ready to bust out of here?"

Bobbie's face split into a wide smile. "You bet your tiny hiney we are."

"We're leaving?" Kensie swung her gaze around the room as the other female attendants moved closer, a ripple of excitement passing through them.

I nodded. "We found the door that leads from the complex. There should be a ship that we can take to get off the moon."

"You can fly a spaceship?" Kensie's eyes widened.

"Nope." I shot a look at Kaos, who hadn't regained much of his composure. "But I'll bet he can, and so can Naz. He's the kalesh, or captain, of their Taori crew."

Bobbie clapped her hands together. "Good enough for me. Let's blow this joint."

She hooked her arm through mine and waved at the other females to follow us.

"Wait!" Kensie's shriek made us all stop in out tracks.

I studied the woman, whose expression was frantic. I'd always sensed she was more frightened than the rest, but was she really going to choose staying behind over the possibility of leaving the arena forever?

She grabbed her collar and yanked at it. "What about these?" Her gaze drifted to my bandaged neck, which was free of the steel ring. "You might not be collared anymore, but the rest of us are. If they catch us trying to leave, the guards will do more than backhand us."

Bobbie's shoulders sagged as the truth of Kensie's words hit her. "She's right. Even if we made it to a ship, they could detonate these and blow our heads off."

Fury at the brutality of the aliens and their twisted moons bubbled up in me like molten lava. "Then we'll have to get them off."

I unhooked my arm from Bobbie's and concentrated on my hands with all my power. I didn't know what I wanted them to shift into, but it had to be strong enough to tear through steel. My fingers burned as the soft flesh morphed into green, scaled hands that looked slick to the touch.

"What the...?" Kensie whispered as all the females gaped at me in shock.

All except for Bobbie, who gave me a knowing look. "You *are* a Lycithian shapeshifter. I *knew* it!"

"Yeah, but long story short, I'm a bit new at shifting." I looked sadly at my hands. "I did not want them to shift into *this*."

"Why not?" Bobbie asked. "It's perfect."

I grimaced at the green scales that had replaced my skin. "How will this help me tear your collars off?"

"You have Xerxen hands."

I looked at her blankly.

"You know," she sighed. "I had to attended one of them. The aliens with the poisonous skin. It should burn right through the metal if you hold the collars tightly."

I almost whooped with happiness. I guess I'd subconsciously known what to shift into after all. Without waiting, I reached over and grabbed Bobbie's collar, being careful not to touch her flesh with my hands.

At first, nothing happened. Then the collar began to sizzle as my acidic flesh ate through it. I squeezed as hard as I could and within seconds, the collar was broken and clattering in prices on the floor. The females gathered eagerly around me, and I worked as quickly as I could, the sharp fragments of steel falling to the floor and scattering around me.

Kensie was the last one to step up to me, but she bit the corner of her bottom lip as I reached for her.

I smiled to reassure her. "I promise not to burn you."

"What happens once we leave?" she whispered to me so that only I could hear her tremulous voice. "I've been here so long I don't know how to live a normal life anymore."

My hands seared through the steel ringing her neck and it fell to her feet. "You're a survivor. I promise you it will be great."

She held my gaze before nodding. "Then let's get the hell out of here."

We ran to the door and Kaos waved all the females through, his jaw so tight that a muscle ticked in the side of it.

"Are you okay?" I asked, not sure if I wanted to know the answer. I'd seen that manic look before, and the Taori appeared to be on the brink of cracking—or letting go.

He didn't speak, instead moving his head up and down jerkily. It would have to do. I ran to the front of the group so I could lead them to the exit, but a roar made me turn.

Two husky guards had rounded the corner and spotted us. Before either could raise an alarm or even raise their batons, Kaos had leapt through the air and landed on them with a ferocity that made us all jump. He rammed them with his horns, stunning them, and then he pummeled them mercilessly.

SUBDUE

When they were both twitching on the floor—alive, but in no shape to pursue us—he swung around and growled. "Go."

I didn't wait for him to say if we should all go, or if we should run from him. I just spun on my heel and took off down the hall as sirens started screaming overhead.

CHAPTER
THIRTY-SEVEN

Naz

My heart thundered as the alarms blared around me. I'd known that my actions couldn't go unnoticed, but I didn't regret anything.

"Even if I don't escape, the cowards won't be able to watch anymore," I said, as I surveyed the wreckage of bodies hanging from the pods, crimson limbs broken and scattered on the floor. The scene was the same in the other rooms filled with pods, although the first room also contained the bodies of the guards who'd stumbled upon me as I'd located the stash of avatars.

My chest heaved from exertion, but I let out a satisfied grunt. The spectators who'd cheered for my death and the death of others had been torn apart by my bare hands. They might not have been able to fight back, but they were far from innocent victims. Without them, there would be no demand for the twisted moons. They deserved to be deprived of their sick amusement.

"If only I could rain this terror on their planet," I muttered as I backed from the last room and raced down the hallway.

I needed to rejoin Tyrria and Kaos, and the other females. Regret twisted my gut that I'd left Tyrria, but there was no one I trusted more than my first officer. He would battle to the death to protect her, and his skills were as deadly as any Taori's. No, Tyrria was in good hands, and now the Xulonian avatars were destroyed.

Rounding a corner, I ran smack into a startled guard. Before he could lift his baton, I leapt at him and spun his neck quickly to snap it. He collapsed to the floor, and I landed in a crouch, my tail swishing. I relished fighting enemies who deserved their fate, and my predatory instincts were awakened as I continued running through the complex and taking out confused guards along the way.

My only regret was that there weren't more Xulonians to punish. I'd thought about taking a detour to visit the director of the battle moon, but it was an indulgence I didn't allow myself. Destroying the avatars with my bare hands had been enough. My priority now was getting to Tyrria and getting her off the moon.

The passageway sloped down, and the ceilings became lower, a sure sign I was closing in on the subterranean level of the complex. I didn't slow until I was skidding to a stop before I crashed into a group of females.

"Naz!" Tyrria's voice rose above the din of the alarms and the hum of the females' nervous chatter. She pushed her way through the group and threw herself in my arms, wrapping her arms around my waist. "You made it."

I curled my arms around her back. "Did you doubt me?"

She peered up. "No, but we need to go."

I nodded, glancing over the heads of the females, and catching the eye of my first officer. His breathing was closer to panting, and the skin that wasn't inked looked flushed. Still, he was managing to control himself among all the females, which meant the fever hadn't consumed him yet.

"You lead the way, Kalesh," he called. "I'll bring up the rear."

I nodded. I would typically be the last Taori out, but I wanted to remain with Tyrria, and getting her onto the escape ship was my highest priority. Of course, my first officer would know that and would preempt any debate.

I pulled Tyrria with me as I moved toward the exit, noticing that none of the females wore collars anymore. There wasn't time to ask how Tyrria and Kaos managed to remove them, but I was impressed by their feat.

The door hidden in the darkened alcove slid open as soon as I touched the inset panel. Instead of bright light streaming in from the outdoors, we were met with another shadowy corridor. I swallowed down my doubt, clutched Tyrria's hand, and waved for the others to follow.

Our fast footfalls and heavy breathing echoed in the low-ceilinged passageway as we ran forward. Tyrria's grip on mine was tight, and I suspected she was as afraid as I was that we weren't running to freedom. If this did not lead to a way out, I didn't know what we would do.

Before I could lose hope, the darkness gave way to a faint glow of light. I squeezed Tyrria's hand and increased my pace until I was nearly blinded by light. My heart soared as we burst from the stone corridor and were outside.

I didn't care that sand was swirling in the air and stinging my skin or that the heat was stifling as sunlight beat down on us. None of that mattered. We'd gotten out.

I put a hand over my eyes and squinted as my eyes adjusted.

"There!" Tyrria extended one arm and pointed to a hulking dark shape. "A ship."

She was right. The ship that had delivered the shipment of fighters was still on the flight deck, and it didn't appear to be preparing for takeoff. That didn't mean there was any time to waste.

I glanced over my shoulder to check that everyone had emerged from the passageway, reassured when I spotted Kaos's head at the back. I raised a fist overhead, and he returned the gesture. Then I spun back around and resumed running across the flight deck and toward the sky ship.

It didn't matter that it was an alien vessel. All ships were similar enough that I knew I could fly it. I growled as I thought about the weaponry the alien ship might possess. If it was anything like the firepower that shot my sky ship from the sky, we should be able to use the ship to inflict some damage.

The ramp to the vessel was down, and I led the way onboard. I didn't hesitate when a Xulonian rushed toward me from the cockpit, knocking the blaster from his hand and snapping his arm. His shrieks of pain were nothing to me as I scooped the blaster from the floor and shot him in the chest. If Tyrria was startled by my lack of mercy, she didn't say anything. Instead, she jumped over the body and followed me deeper into the ship.

"It's big enough to hold all of us," she said, relief obvious in her voice.

I released her hand. "Make sure the other females are safely on board. I'm going to fire up the engines."

She nodded and ran in the opposite direction. I paused and spotted Kaos running up the ramp before I hurried to the cockpit. Good. We were all accounted for. Time to escape and enact some revenge.

I reached the cockpit and flopped into the pilot's chair. It had been many moons since I'd taken the helm of such a small sky ship, but flying was not a skill that was easy to forget. I swept my fingers across the console, grinning when it lit up and buttons overhead were illuminated. Using instinct, I engaged the engines, my pulse quickening when the sky ship rumbled to life under my feet.

Then the first explosion hit the hull.

CHAPTER
THIRTY-EIGHT

Tyrria

The blast knocked me sideways as I waved the other females toward the back of the ship. None of us wanted to go in the makeshift cells that the Xulonians had clearly used to transport captives, but luckily there were also some cramped quarters and even a medical bay. I ran back to the center of the vessel and peered out the ramp that was still open even though the engine was engaged. A fleet of guards were running toward us as they fired, even though they were too corpulent to be fast.

Kaos stood at the top of the ramp, and Kensie was behind him, clutching his waistband to keep from falling. With one arm, he held her behind him and with the other he snatched a blaster from the wall and fired at the approaching guards. The Taori looked even wilder and more like a beast than Naz had when he'd been in the battle ring, but that wasn't a bad thing considering we might have to shoot our way off the moon.

I staggered past them as the ship lifted off the ground with the ramp still open and blaster fire ricocheting off the metal hull.

"Close the ramp," I yelled as I entered the cockpit.

Naz didn't look back at me, but he did nod and scan the shiny console before tapping it. Even with the engines engaging and the weapons fire, I heard the mechanical groan of the ramp lifting. I grabbed the back of the pilot's chair for balance as the alien ship thrust into the air, sand kicking up around it.

Now that we were outside the complex and rising above it, I could see that there were rolling sand dunes surrounding the impressive arena, which looked almost like an elaborate, tiered cake, with all of its colored domes. I marveled at how beautiful it looked from the outside, and what horrors were contained within.

Naz's fingers danced across the console, and we lifted off the moon even faster, the large domed roof of the oblong arena shrinking beneath us until it vanished entirely, and we were flying about the cloud cover. As we soared through the atmosphere and shot into space, the ship's alerts started wailing.

Naz frowned and flicked more buttons overhead, but he froze when a pair of ships that looked like the one we were in materialized in front of us.

He narrowed his eyes at them. "Time to see what kind of weapons we have."

Symbols flashed across the screen, and he hesitated, his hands hovering over the console. "Those are Taori letters."

"Xulonian ships are sending you a message in Taori?" I gaped at the ships flanking us. "Do you think they have your ship mates prisoner, and are forcing them to send messages in your language?"

He craned his neck to look at me. "Now I do."

"Sorry. I'm used to worst-case scenarios."

Naz released a tortured breath. "Even if that is the case, I must answer."

Before I could ask him if he was crazy for accepting the hail, he tapped the console. Our view of the enemy ships vanished, and a familiar-looking alien filled the view screen.

"Torst?"

The dark-haired Taori with silver horns and scruffy cheeks smiled, his eyes closing for a beat while his blue eyes shone. "Kalesh Naz. I did not think my gaze would rest on you again."

Naz's shoulder sagged. "I feared I might not see any of my Taori brothers again."

Another Taori face appeared on the screen. "Kalesh! I knew you would not be beckoned by the sultry whispers of death into the shadowland."

"Skard." Naz laughed, a deep joyful sound I hadn't heard from him. "I should have expected that my navigator would find his way out of any predicament."

The Taori hitched one shoulder. "It was not as simple as routing my way through a galaxy, but I am well. Daiken is also with us."

"How...?" Naz started to ask, then shook his head. "There will be time for that later. First, we must find the rest of our Immortals."

"We're on it." A dark-haired female pushed Skard aside. "More ships are joining us to take down the Xulonians."

I leaned over Naz's shoulder, recognizing the woman on the screen. "You're from the imperial transport."

She grinned. "Carly. I was security chief. And you were our mysterious cargo. Glad to see you alive and kicking."

My face warmed at the reminder that I'd been cargo intended to be delivered to an imperial commander. "I'm no one's cargo anymore." I cut my gaze to Naz. "But I am his."

The first Taori's dark brows lifted, but he didn't comment.

"I assume you have a plan of attack?" Naz asked, as he snaked an arm around my waist to pull me closer to him.

"I'm sending you the plans on an encrypted channel and in Taori code. For now, follow us so we can hide your ship from Xulonian sensors."

"Understood." Naz drew in a deep breath. "Into the valley of death ride the Ten Thousand."

"We are Taori," the warriors on the screen intoned.

"We are the Immortals," they all said together, in deep voices that made chills skitter down my arms.

With a nod, Naz closed the channel and steered the ship behind the other two, skirting around the moon and establishing an orbit on the dark side of the battle moon.

Then he sat back and pulled me fully into his lap. "Did you mean what you said?"

"What?" I tried to sit up, but he kept me pinned down.

"That you're mine. Did you mean that?"

I'd said it so impulsively I hadn't thought before the words had spilled from my mouth. But I knew in my gut, they were true. "I meant them."

"Even...?"

"You mean even after I let my insecurity make me stupid, got angry, and tried to kill you?"

The corner of his mouth twitched up. "I never lied to you, Tyrria. Only to them, and only to protect you."

"I know." My throat tightened. "I'm still learning that not all men lie to me and want to use me."

He cupped my face in one hand. "I am bound by your eyes and to your heart, Tyrria. My soul is yours until it crosses into the shadowland." After repeating the words he'd said to me in the battle ring, he dragged one rough thumb across my bottom lip with a hum of desire. "If I need to spend my life proving that to you, so be it."

My breath caught in my chest. "Maybe not your *entire* life."

He chuckled low. "Your concession is appreciated." He brushed his lips across mine. "Maybe there's something I can do to convince you of my devotion."

I cocked my head at him and gave him a wicked smile. "I can think of a few things."

He ran his hand up through my hair and pulled my mouth down to his in a hard, claiming kiss that I felt all the way to my toes. I wound my arms around his neck and surrendered myself to the feel of my hands braced against his hard chest and his lips devouring mine. I slipped my hands up to his horns, my fingertips brushing the ridged stripes, as I savored his deep-throated growl.

"There you are!"

I tore my lips from Naz and shot a look at Bobbie as she stumbled into the cockpit. "Can this wait?"

"I wish it could." She gnawed on her bottom lip. "You know how Kensie was the last one on the ship? Well, we can't find her."

Naz straightened. "A female is missing?"

"But I saw her inside when I was running to the cockpit." I glanced at Naz. "She was behind your first officer."

"About that." Bobbie winced. "He's gone, too."

CHAPTER THIRTY-NINE

Kaos

The wind buffeted my body and tossed my hair around my face as the sky ship lifted off the ground. The female with the brown curls clung to me from behind as the ship rocked from side to side and blaster fire pinged off the steel hull of the vessel. She was the last one up the ramp in front of me and the first shots had been fired as we'd reached the top. There'd been no time to push her farther inside, before I had to turn and snatch a weapon from the wall and return fire. Still, I curled one arm behind me to hold her steady as we rose into the air.

The kalesh's mate—the one he'd looked at as if she belonged to no one else in the universe—ran past us and toward the cockpit. Then the engines fired again, kicking the ship back, and the female behind me slipped, her feet skittering from beneath her she slid from my grasp and between my legs before I could tighten my grip. Without a second thought, I dove for her as she tumbled down the ramp. I reached her but my momentum was too great, and we both flew from the ship. I curled my body around hers as we both plummeted through the air, the rushing wind making it impossible to scream.

The sky ship hadn't lifted very high from the ground, but I still closed my eyes and braced myself for impact on the hard surface of the flight deck. Instead, we landed in a sand dune, rolling together down one side before coming to a stop at the bottom.

I lay sprawled, face-up, as I attempted to regain the breath that had been knocked from me. The sun was brutal as it shone down on my skin, and the air was dry and hot, making it hard to take deep breaths.

The sound of the blaster fire was muffled, and as I pushed myself onto my elbows, I saw that we were hidden from the arena complex by the sand dune we'd rolled down. Tipping my head back, I saw the alien sky ship that held my kalesh and the females I'd helped rescue. Instead of returning to the surface for us, the ramp clamped shut and it continued to ascend higher in the air.

"They're leaving!" The female I'd tried to save before she'd fallen from the open ramp was struggling to stand beside me, her face stricken as she gaped at the departing vessel. "They're leaving without us!"

Even though her screams couldn't yet be heard above the weapons fire and roaring of the engine, I couldn't risk her giving away our position. We might not be on the ship escaping, but at least we were not prisoners inside the arena. I would not be anyone's captive again.

I threw myself on the female, clamping a thick hand over

her mouth and flattening my body to hers. "They will return for us."

Her eyes were wide as she stared up at me and struggled to push me off her.

The movements of her small body beneath mine sent unwanted pulses of pleasure through me and awakened the barely dormant fever. I closed my eyes, cursing in the ancient tongue of my ancestors as I tried to fight it off.

I could not be stricken with the Quaibyn. Not now. Not when I'd just been stranded on a barren, alien moon with a very scared and very pretty female.

The noises of the departing sky ship faded as did the sounds of blasters being fired. The creature under me went still as rough voices drifted to us from just on the other side of the dune. The cruel guards were so close they'd only need to crest the sand to see us lying in the valley.

I held my breath and lowered my head so that it was almost nestled in her neck as I waited for the guards to return to the arena. There were a few dark grumbles and loud shouts of displeasure, but then they stomped away, their footfall fading as they left.

I let out a grateful sigh. In all the chaos of the sky ship taking off and them shooting, they hadn't seen us fall and land in the desert.

Then I allowed myself a breath, inhaling the sweet scent of the female I was restraining. My body stiffened as a rumble built in my chest. I trembled with desire, my flesh on fire as I dragged the tip of my tongue up the length of her neck. Then I growled and felt her shudder beneath me.

We were all alone in the desert, and there was no one to quench the fever that turned me into a desperate, rutting beast. Only her.

SUBDUE

~

THANK YOU FOR READING SUBDUE! Want to know what happens to Kaos and Kensie when they're left on the alien moon? Don't miss STORM, book five in the series.

Enslaved to the alien gladiators. Trapped on a harsh alien moon. Stranded with an alien warrior who may be as dangerous as my former captors.

One-click STORM

~

This book has been edited and proofed, but typos are like little gremlins that like to sneak in when we're not looking. If you spot a typo, please report it to: tana@tanastone.com
Thank you!!

ALSO BY TANA STONE

Warriors of the Drexian Academy:

LEGACY

LOYALTY

THE SKY CLAN OF THE TAORI:

SUBMIT (also available in AUDIO)

STALK (also available on AUDIO)

SEDUCE (also available on AUDIO)

SUBDUE

STORM

Inferno Force of the Drexian Warriors:

IGNITE (also available on AUDIO)

SCORCH (also available on AUDIO)

BURN (also available on AUDIO)

BLAZE (also available on AUDIO)

FLAME (also available on AUDIO)

COMBUST

The Tribute Brides of the Drexian Warriors Series:

TAMED (also available in AUDIO)

SEIZED (also available in AUDIO)

EXPOSED (also available in AUDIO)

RANSOMED (also available in AUDIO)

FORBIDDEN (also available in AUDIO)

BOUND (also available in AUDIO)

JINGLED (A Holiday Novella) (also in AUDIO)

CRAVED (also available in AUDIO)

STOLEN (also available in AUDIO)

SCARRED (also available in AUDIO)

ALIEN & MONSTER ONE-SHOTS:

ROGUE (also available in AUDIO)

VIXIN: STRANDED WITH AN ALIEN

SLIPPERY WHEN YETI

CHRISTMAS WITH AN ALIEN

YOOL

Raider Warlords of the Vandar Series:

POSSESSED (also available in AUDIO)

PLUNDERED (also available in AUDIO)

PILLAGED (also available in AUDIO)

PURSUED (also available in AUDIO)

PUNISHED (also available on AUDIO)

PROVOKED (also available in AUDIO)

PRODIGAL (also available in AUDIO)

PRISONER

PROTECTOR

PRINCE

The Barbarians of the Sand Planet Series:

BOUNTY (also available in AUDIO)

CAPTIVE (also available in AUDIO)

TORMENT (also available on AUDIO)

TRIBUTE (also available as AUDIO)

SAVAGE (also available in AUDIO)

CLAIM (also available on AUDIO)

CHERISH: A Holiday Baby Short (also available on AUDIO)

PRIZE (also available on AUDIO)

SECRET

RESCUE (appearing first in PETS IN SPACE #8)

All the TANA STONE books available as audiobooks!

INFERNO FORCE OF THE DREXIAN WARRIORS:

IGNITE on AUDIBLE

SCORCH on AUDIBLE

BURN on AUDIBLE

BLAZE on AUDIBLE

FLAME on AUDIBLE

RAIDER WARLORDS OF THE VANDAR:

POSSESSED on AUDIBLE

PLUNDERED on AUDIBLE

PILLAGED on AUDIBLE

PURSUED on AUDIBLE

PUNISHED on AUDIBLE

PROVOKED on AUDIBLE

BARBARIANS OF THE SAND PLANET

BOUNTY on AUDIBLE

CAPTIVE on AUDIBLE

TORMENT on AUDIBLE

TRIBUTE on AUDIBLE

SAVAGE on AUDIBLE

CLAIM on AUDIBLE

CHERISH on AUDIBLE

TRIBUTE BRIDES OF THE DREXIAN WARRIORS

TAMED on AUDIBLE

SEIZED on AUDIBLE

EXPOSED on AUDIBLE

RANSOMED on AUDIBLE

FORBIDDEN on AUDIBLE

BOUND on AUDIBLE

JINGLED on AUDIBLE

CRAVED on AUDIBLE

STOLEN on AUDIBLE

SCARRED on AUDIBLE

SKY CLAN OF THE TAORI

SUBMIT on AUDIBLE

STALK on AUDIBLE

SEDUCE on AUDIBLE

About the Author

Tana Stone is a USA Today bestselling sci-fi romance author who loves sexy aliens and independent heroines. Her favorite superhero is Thor (with Aquaman a close second because, well, Jason Momoa), her favorite dessert is key lime pie (okay, fine, *all* pie), and she loves Star Wars and Star Trek equally. She still laments the loss of *Firefly*.

She has one husband, two teenagers, two dogs, and three neurotic cats. She sometimes wishes she could teleport to a holographic space station like the one in her tribute brides series (or maybe vacation at the oasis with the sand planet barbarians). :-)

She loves hearing from readers! Email her any questions or comments at tana@tanastone.com.

Want to hang out with Tana in her private Facebook group? Join on all the fun at: https://www.facebook.com/groups/tanastonestributes/

Copyright © 2022 by Broadmoor Books

Cover Design by Croco Designs

Editing by Tanya Saari

All rights reserved.

No part of this book may be reproduced in any form or by any electronic or mechanical means, including information storage and retrieval systems, without written permission from the author, except for the use of brief quotations in a book review.

This is a work of fiction. Names, characters, places, and incidents are the products of the author's imagination or are used fictitiously and are not to be construed as real. Any resemblance to actual events, locales, organizations, or persons, living or dead, is entirely coincidental.

Printed in Dunstable, United Kingdom